T0077723

Resuming HISTORY

SARAH SYED

PARTRIDGE
A Penguin Random House Company

To order additional copies of this book, contact
Toll Free 800 101 2657 (Singapore)
Toll Free 1 800 81 7340 (Malaysia)
orders.singapore@partridgepublishing.com

www.partridgepublishing.com/singapore

Contents

To Nana and Nani

Author's Note

The images provided do not exactly match the description; they are there to help the reader imagine the scenario in a better way.

Book of Dreams

Dreams of a pendant
Pendant of red
Red as a heart
Heart of ink
Ink of Alex
Alex with an aura
Aura that Jett seeks
Seek not get
Get in his dreams
Dreams of a queen
Queen that imprisons

–Akhtar Naveed Syed

Chapter 1

I find myself running on a long never ending road, my feet moving on their own accord. Where am I going? Even I don't know. My eyes are shut tight, my mind wishing that everything disappears. Its pitch dark, where did the lights go??

My foot suddenly crashes into something hard 'BAAM'. I held my breath, waiting for my nose to break when I land face first on the solid ground. But the pain never came, instead I found myself standing in a dimly lit hallway with lockers; ALOT of lockers.

Wait, what's happening? I'm not supposed to be here. I don't want to be here.

Someone pushes me into a locker; my back hits the cold metal causing pain to spread all over my spine and ribs. Suddenly, I feel something cold and slimy run down my face. I reach up and touch my head finding huge blobs of pasta tangled in my hair.

What in the world is going on?!?!

He was laughing an evil laugh, the sound booming all around the hallway. Everyone was laughing with him, making fun of me. I clasped my hands over my ears, trying to shut out their sounds. I want to cry.

"Alexandra, wake up!! We're going be late. GETTTT UUUUUPPPP!!!!!!!"

It was the same dream again. Why can't he leave me alone, now I'm sweating, ugghh!!

All of a sudden, she yanked my blanket causing me to fall over and land on my stomach. Rolling over I sat up, my back against the side of my bed.

"Oww, Mom" I whined rubbing my knee," five more minutes, please. And its Alex NOT Alexandra," I said the last part sternly while getting up and snuggling back into my comfy white blanket. I HATE getting up early. I'm not a morning person, unlike the rest of my family.

I would have been someone like them 4 years ago. Always waking up at 5:30 in the morning when my sister jumped on my bed singing -more like shouting- some crazy Disney tale song.

But not anymore, now I am different, I have changed my name and my personality -everyone- my new friends and all my new teachers know me as Alex. I know it's a boyish name, but it sounds much better than Alexandra. No offence to all the Alexandras of the world. I've become more grown up and less scared of the world and all its bullies. If you haven't understood yet, let me explain this to you.

When I was younger, from the first day of pre-school, me and my friends, we'd been bullied by the biggest group of jerks. I HATE them. But why remember them now, they were in my past, life is moving and I've moved on.

Today is my first morning here, back at home. I've missed this place more than I thought I had. I missed my room, my bed, heck I even missed my sister's stupid green parrot. That thing makes the most random comments ever.

I've missed my Mom and her strict rules. It's not like she's a not-fun-mother, it's just that she likes us to be organized and always on time. I've missed Dad and his crazy obsession with plants. Dad loves growing plants; I think he started this after we watched *'Wall.e'*. Dad says that his plants will someday save us all from dying. I do believe him you know; we did learn this in biology back in grade 9, at school.

But the one person I missed the most is my little sister. She is the most adorable kid no one cannot miss. It wasn't her cuteness that I missed, it was her. She used to be so little but acted very grownup. Sierra used to tell me all her secrets and problems. I was some kind of therapist to her who can solve all her problems. She used to help me study; it was more like me studying while she asked questions about the stuff she heard me memorize. I used to explain them to her and Sierra used to hear me attentively even though I'm sure she didn't get a word I used to talk about. Sierra is 8 years younger than me. She's 10 now - or today.

Even though I Skype with them every week and called them every single day I couldn't stop missing them. Video call or any type of call can't be as good as talking to someone face-to-face.

"Alexandra wake up NOW or I'm going to forget you're 18,"my Mom threatened. When we were little kids, me and Sierra, we used to act like we hated waking up in the morning. Sometimes Mom used to get mad really quick and either splash us with a mug of water or drag us under an icy shower. Our slow, sleepy reflexes used to fail us and allowed our Mom to do what she wanted.

It may sound funny, but it's not if you can't strangle the person who's done it to you. I hate it when this happens.

Ignoring what she called me, this time I stood up and dragged my tired body to the bathroom. My room has an attached bath with purple tiles on the floor and alternate white and purple ones on the walls. I got myself a white towel and picked an outfit for today's occasion. Then I jumped under the cold shower. It took me a few minutes to adjust to the waters temperature. After I felt less shaken up by the coldness, I took all my time to scrub and get clean then I changed into a pair of dark skinny jeans and a loose pink t-shirt that said *'Always Think Positive'* in white cursive font on the front.

I stuffed my pocket with my hot pink headphones together with my phone and some money. I applied some chapstick and made my now almost dry hair into a side braid. Grabbing one of my favorite books from the shelf I went up to Sierra's room. Her door was wide open and the bed was made. She's not home just like I had been told last night.

Today is Sierra's birthday, she's turning 10. Mom sent her for a sleep over last night; she told me that both my parents and Sierra's best friend have decided to throw her a surprise party. I think I'm part of this surprise because Sierra doesn't know that I'm back. Sierra and I, we used to be really close but then after I left, we slowly grew apart. Mom told me that Sierra became friend's with her now-best-friend an year after I left. She was very alone and her friend helped her.

It's not like I don't feel guilty because I do, but I had to leave. I couldn't live the life I was living. I had had enough of living in the shadows, being bullied around for no reason. Everyone at school leaving out my friends, the teachers and the principal hated me. There was this girl, the popular one at school, she didn't hate me but she did pity me. I could see it in her eyes and on her face. I HATE to be pitied.

Pulling myself out of my thoughts I made my way to the stairs. I can hear Mom and Dad downstairs. Mom is making everyone help pack the picnic baskets. I jogged down to the kitchen, murmured a *'Good Morning'*, and grabbed the beach ball from the dining table together with a large blanket and two pillows. Then I headed out to my Dad's red Mini Cooper. My Dad has the weirdest choices but I always end up loving them. Dad bought this car last year when I was still away. Our Mini is dark red with 3 white stripes in the middle all the way on the car. It's a beautiful car, one of my favorites. I opened the car and stuffed everything I was carrying in the backseat. Then I started it, the engine roared to life alerting my parents that we were getting late. One after the other I saw them both scurry towards the car each carrying a basket, Dad also carrying a cool box while Mom had another blanket tucked under her arm.

Mom took shotgun while Dad drove and I was stuck in the backseat with all the food, blankets and pillows. Right now we were on the highway. The party which only consists of my family and Sierra's friends' is supposed to be at a beach house my parents have rented. Sierra's school took her here last year. She told me on Skype. I can still remember how happy she was when she was telling me about the little adventures she had that day. I remember her saying *'You can never leave this place without having an adventure'*.

As we neared our destination I could smell the salty water from my open window. The wind hit my face as I leaned to look outside. I shivered from its coldness and closed my window; I really don't feel like getting sick on my first day back home. When we reached all I could see were grey rocks and a few birds flying from one palm tree to the other. I could hear birds but wait, is that a frog croaking, what is a frog doing near a beach?

Upon seeing my confused expression Mom spoke up and explained. "It's not really a beach house or a beach. We're near a lagoon but Sierra's little mind still thinks it's a small beach." I smiled at what Mom said and helped them pick up the supplies. We then started making our way over the rocks. As I crossed them and reached to the other side the most beautiful and picturesque scenery was laid in front of my eyes. Never ever have I seen a place such mesmerizing.

The water was blue, more like dark turquoise, while the sand was white and soft. The light breeze I could feel made everything even better. There was a small waterfall far ahead between two completely green, moss covered rocky hills. There were around twenty

Sarah Syed

palm trees around us. Some were even growing right out of the water. The birds were chirping while hidden frogs and crickets made funny sounds. There were a thousand flowers, some indigo and the others a creamy white. Now I know why Sierra likes this place. A place like this screams of adventure and mystery. The lagoon is connected to a spring which is probably somehow connected to the sea. I could tell that from the fresh salty smell that was still filling my senses.

I followed Dad to the small hut or a beach house as Sierra called it. It wasn't a luxurious place but it had the feeling of coziness making me feel at home. As I looked around I saw two chairs lying in front of a small fire place. There was a small stove in a corner and a cabinet filled with utensils. A couple of foldable beach chairs were lying under the cabinet. One of the hut's walls was made of glass allowing a lot of sunshine to pass through and light up the whole place. I moved to where the baskets were lying on the steps outside our cabin. I opened the first one I saw and pulled out a hand pump with a packet of balloons, then walked back in to start decorating the place. It was getting late; Sierra would be here in 30 minutes.

I filled the balloons using the pump while Dad blew them up himself. Mom was busy setting up our brunch which consisted of chicken sandwiches, fruits and a variety of drinks. My stomach grumbled due to the lack of breakfast, I went and picked a juicy red apple then continued hanging the *Happy Birthday* sign above the picnic table. Dad helped me secure it in place so that it doesn't fall and ruin the cake which was placed right underneath it.

Mom hung a huge poster of Sierra's favorite band on the opposite wall to the table. She then proceeded by icing the cake with fluffy sky blue cream. There were 10 minutes left for Sierra to arrive. I looked around and agreed that we had done the work well. The walls were decorated with heart shaped balloons while the floor was scattered with round ones. The wooden picnic table was now covered with a magenta velvet cloth with the food lying on top of it. The drinks were crowding on a table outside the cabin. Everything looked in place. Perfect!

Just as we finished with the final touches I heard an engine outside. I climbed out the back door and hid behind some bushes. Maybelle, Sierra's friend is supposed to bring her in the hut and then I'm supposed to enter from the back door and surprise her. Mom's idea not mines!

As I made myself comfortable behind the bushes I slowly heard the engine die down and footsteps could be heard. There were girls talking, Sierra and Maybelle. Then I heard heavier footsteps behind, probably Maybelle's parents. After a few minutes shouts erupted, everyone was screaming '*Surprise*'. After a few minutes a little girl around 10 or 11 walked out the back door towards the bush I was hiding behind.

I've heard Sierra describe her so many times that I instantly recognized her. It was Maybelle. She wore a yellow knee length frock with a red beanie on top of her brunette curls. She had greyish-blue eyes, a very familiar shade might I add. She stopped and looked around then whispered, "Andy can you please come out, it's time to surprise Sierra." Sierra calls me Andy so I assume that is what she has told her friend.

I stood up and brushed the dust off my pants. Fixing the wrinkles on my shirt I made my way to the little girl. When I reached her I stretched out my arm and greeted her with a small *'Hello'*. She shook my hand, "Hi!! I'm Maybelle, but you can call me May, that's what Sierra and everyone else calls me", she whispered excitedly. She had a bubbly high pitched voice, it sounded cute on a girl like her. She then grabbed my hand and pulled me to the door. I followed her and waited for Dad's signal. We stood there quietly; well I stood quietly while she blabbered happily about something Sierra had told her about. Her eyes were twinkling with excitement. I like this kid; she's just like my Sierra. I stood there patiently listening to May, after almost fifteen minutes of standing there we heard three consecutive taps; I think that was the signal.

I slowly opened the door and stepped in, Maybelle tailing behind me. Both Sierra's and a tall broad shouldered figure's backs were facing me. He was covering her eyes while she waited for her surprise impatiently. He whispered something inaudible making her laugh. Just as I shouted surprise, he let her go. She turned around, her eyes the size of saucers. First she stared at me in shock, then she came running to me and engulfed me in a bone crushing bear hug. I closed my eyes and twirled the little laughing thing around. God, I love her so, so much. She is very, very important to me.

I bent down to her level kissing the tip of her nose, "Happy Birthday Ree," I wished my little sister. "I'm sorry I couldn't get you a gift, but I promise to get you anything you like." The twinkle in her eyes disappeared for a moment when I told her about the gift but instantly lightened up again after hearing the last part. I really didn't have any time to buy her something, but I'm sure we can make some time one of these days.

Note to self: Take Ree to the mall.

I stood up and looked around at everyone. They traveled from one person to the other until they stopped on the last two.

What are *THEY* doing here?

The fear in me started building up again. It was him and his sister. She was standing like a statue, completely petrified like Hermione was in *Chamber of Secrets*. Her long strawberry blonde hair was tied in a high ponytail. She still has her perfect model like body but something about her felt different. A good type of different, if you may ask.

But he stood there as if he didn't recognize me. How come he doesn't know who I am? Oh right, I've changed my style. No more nerdy glasses or messy curly hair or hiding behind shadows. I looked very different now. But I can't look that unrecognizable, can I? He's basically smiling, no, more like grinning at me. He waved at me awkwardly.

"Hi," he said.

Chapter 2

'*Hi*', that's all he has to say. I mean, we are meeting after I don't know how many years and all he says is '*Hi*'. I stood staring at him for almost 3 minutes. My eyes wide, jaw hanging and mouth half open. When he saw my behavior he backed away. I think, he thinks I am crazy or something. His eyes narrowed, searching my face for any resemblance. As soon as his dark orbs met my green ones, I averted my gaze down to my constantly shuffling feet. I was sure if we kept the eye contact for a minute more he would have known who I am.

I kept looking at my brown boots, acting as though I had discovered long lost treasure on them. An awkward silence passed. Everyone's eyes were on me, I knew that without even looking. I opened my mouth to find myself squeak a short '*Hello*'. As soon as I had embarrassed myself to death, I ran out to where Ree and May were playing. I jumped down the front stairs looking around.

I found them near the end of the lagoon. I walked, no wait, I almost ran and sat beside Ree with Maybelle sitting opposite to us. The girls were chattering happily. "Hey guys, so what are you doing?" I literally forced the sound out of me trying to look casual. They hadn't witnessed what happened inside. "We're using rocks and pebbles to make a castle for the Princess'," May said pointing to her and Ree's dolls then to a pile of moist stones.

I started helping make the walls of their castle, trying my best to forget what was awaiting me inside. Just as we were done balancing the stones on the second wall I heard light steps walking on wood. I turned around to find Fiona walking towards me. She was wearing dark green skinny jeans with a beige sweater. Her hair tied in a high ponytail and her ears carrying tiny *'m&m's'* as earrings. She looked pretty as always; with her high cheekbones, flawless fair skin and dark grey-blue eyes. She sat beside May and turned towards us.

"So......you're back??" She asked hesitation clear in her voice.

"Umm, yeah, so......how are you and your bro....... I mean everyone else??" I said.

She stared at me with calculating eyes trying to understand if I meant what I asked. She knows that I hate or hated this place, and them. So why would I be asking something like that. Her mouth opened her voice soft and apologetic.

"I'm very sorry about my brother and his behavior all these years. He just thought that you are someone you aren't. I'm sorry."

"It's okay," that's all I could say after hearing a sudden, might I add, very weird apology. Fiona, she was acting differently. I met her sad eyes and smiled, extending my arm I took hold of her right hand. I gave it a small squeeze to show that I appreciated what she said. She deciphered a small lopsided smile, and just like that we started talking as if we were old best friends.

Okay, so today wasn't going that bad.

I think I had said that a bit too early. Just then Jett stormed out of the hut. He looked at me, his face contorted in disgust, just like old times. Instead of joining us on the ground -like everyone else- he turned his body and moved to sit on the hood of his car. I noticed him giving us confused glances, probably thinking why the heck is Fiona, his twin sister, talking and laughing with me. Both his sisters' backs were facing him while I and my sister had a good view of him and his very expensive sports car. I took in his appearance; he was wearing ripped faded jeans with a white T-shirt. His muscles can be seen unlike when we were younger and still kids. He was wearing a grey beanie on his straight black messy hair. He had a few stubbles on his face making him look older and manlier. He is good-looking, like the rest of his siblings.

Before he could catch me staring, I turned back to the miniature castle of stones. Right then, Fiona and I were deciding on how to make the roof stay up while the little girls were fetching more pebbles. There were stones everywhere but the best ones -according to Ree and May- were located somewhere near the waterfall under the water. Mom had let us go in, the water's quite shallow and the current was in the hut's direction, not allowing anyone to float away. We know how to swim but Mom gets concerned when it comes to water or anything sporty like football, basketball, swimming, excreta. When I used to play basketball for the school team, instead of saying encouraging words like *'You can do it'* or *'Go and win this thing'*, Mom used to *order* me to not get hurt or break my leg or get hit by the ball.

We were talking about random stuff like shopping and TV programs when suddenly Fiona asked me where I had been the last four years. I wanted to avoid the question, it was too embarrassing and senseless, but then she said I could trust her. Does she look worthy for my trust? Yes, she looked worthy; so I told her. I told her that I left after the day Jett reached an extreme in embarrassing me about my appearance, my friends and everything else. I was angry but I didn't show it, instead I ran away from my fears and hid in a boring, old boarding school. I didn't leave the place even to visit my parents or friends. I stayed there until graduation which was last week and then I'm free to go anywhere. I'm back home for summer and after that I'll be moving out to college.

Just as I finished my tale, Maybelle came running towards us, a dozen tiny rocks in her pockets and hands. She dropped them at our folded legs and ran back with a bucket in her hand. I looked over Fiona's shoulder. Ree was telling Maybelle something. I think that *'something'* was underwater. They both started jumping up and down, just as they were about to run our way, Sierra's foot slipped and she screamed. I stood up at top speed but Jett beat me by sprinting to them first.

I reached them and joined Maybelle who was trying to help. She looked scared. Sierra's foot was stuck between two huge boulders and Jett was trying to pull it out as gently as possible. Tears were streaming down her face. She looked in so much pain. Both me and Jett worked together to accomplish our delicate mission of get-Ree-out-without-her-getting-hurt. As soon as her foot was set free from its captivity, blood started oozing out of the many cuts she had gotten.

Jett picked her up and carried her to the blanket we were sitting on. Mom and Dad were out by now, watching the show. Mom was wearing a worried expression while Dad looked extremely angry. Jett set her down and everyone crowded around. Mom bent down and picked up her bleeding foot while I hushed her, she was crying furiously but had now calmed down to hiccups. Mom and Jett cleaned her wound and bandaged it after applying some medicine. Jett's face had become soft and his fingers were gently stroking Ree's arm. He was whispering encouraging words in her ear making her smile.

A pang of jealousy hit me. I'm her sister. I was supposed to be doing the comforting work, not him. Stupid boy.

Suddenly Ree started grinning, her lips spread across her face and pearly white teeth showing. I stared at her, a weird feeling spreading across my chest. Did she bump her head and go mad? Who would be smiling in a situation like this? No, maybe it's just me hallucinating like our late grandmother. Yeah that must be it. But then Maybelle started grinning too, the same mischievous smile on her face. Now I was a bit curious. What's going on?

To everyone's surprise they both shouted the same words at the same time, "We found treasure!!"

Okay.....so I wasn't expecting that, I expected something more like *'Your faces were hilarious when Sierra got hurt'* or *'We were pranking you'*. Who thought about treasure?

Wait.... did they just say *TREASURE* as in gold and lots of money. Oh my god, we are going to be -as if we're not already are- rich!! I wanted to dance but of course, I didn't. People would think I am crazier than I already am.

Everyone except me and Ree stood up and started following May. I looked at Sierra asking for her permission, she nodded to where May stood beckoning me to go behind her friend.

As I approached the huddled group I saw Dad and Jett working on moving a huge boulder. His lean muscles contracted at every movement making me admire his strength. Just as I reached, Dad moved out of the water and on to the rocks from where Mom was watching. You thought I was talking about Jett, didn't you? Never in a million years is that going to happen.

I moved into the water, Fiona tailing behind me. Together we both helped Jett move one heavy rock after the other. Something was shining from underneath the cramped rocks. As we neared our so called treasure, it became clearer of what it was. It was a box, probably made of gold from the radiant shine it was reflecting. It was cuboid in shape and had a hollow oval in between that had words carved in perfect cursive handwriting. I couldn't make out the words but the picture of the oval looked very familiar, as if I had seen it somewhere.

Me and Fiona, we jumped onto the rocks and made ourselves comfortable while Jett swam down to get the box. After a few seconds he emerged from the surface, his hands carrying a bright golden box which looked a lot like a briefcase, minus the handle. Jett swam out to the shore and we followed behind to get a better look at what our discovery was.

The way Jett carried the box made it look heavy, even for a strong guy like him. I went and sat opposite to him with the mystery box between us. Like always, he decided to act childish and pulled the box towards him, a scowl on his face. Mom and Dad stood behind kneeling by my shoulder to get a better look. Maybelle had helped Sierra to get closer and was also waiting for us to open the box.

Jett hovered his hand over the box making us all impatient and more curious with every second. He then started moving his hand on the surface, his fingers delicately brushing over the funny shapes and carvings that covered the lid. His eyes were moving over the foreign language, as if he was reading and understanding the words it spoke. He slowly reached the hollow oval in the middle, his fingers grazing the writing on it. The handwriting looked familiar but not enough to make me remember where I'd seen it. Jett abruptly looked up, his wide, shocked eyes meeting my confused ones. His pupils slowly moved down my face stopping and zoning on something between my collar bones. What the heck? First he hates me and now he was staring at me?

I tilted my head downwards to look at what had interested him so much. There was nothing, just my shirt and my pendant. Pendant? Just as I thought of the word a pair of fingers brushed my neck picking the ruby pendant in their hand. My head jolted up in surprise. I smacked Jett's fingers and jumped back giving him a deathly look. How dare he come near me? What's his problem?

He glared at me then turned to Fiona whispering frantically in her ear. Her face looked like she didn't agree but then after a short while of twin telepathy she nodded and turned to my family. She glanced at Maybelle who carried the same worried look. She then turned her gaze back to us, particularly settling her eyes on me.

Fiona cleared her throat and started speaking, "This box is important to us, we'd like to open it privately," she said. It's important to us too; we found it together if she doesn't remember. I wanted to say that out loud but her shaky voice told me to keep listening. "We would like to take it home and......." She trailed off, not wanting to continue. Jett took ahold of the talk and finished what his sister had started, "We want that pendant."

His voice was demanding and cold which made my anger meter to raise to the level it shattered to pieces. First they don't share the box we found *TOGETHER*, and now he wants *MY* pendant without any good reason. NO!!

"Who do you think you are?" I said, my voice rising with every word. I was furious beyond imagination. I gave the twins a disgusted glare, showing them I refused their request -more like command- then I turned around and stalked off to hut slamming the wooden door behind me.

I could hear voices outside, frantically discussing something. I was too tired to eavesdrop on their conversation. After a few minutes I heard an engine and the door to the hut opened. Dad walked in, Sierra in his arms and Mom behind them. Dad placed Ree on a chair and both parents turned to me. They looked exhausted. I assume the *discussion* didn't go well. Dad sighed, "They took the box with them."

Chapter 3

One week later

"What should I get you?" No answer. "Alex.....
ALEX," I snapped out of my thoughts -which
unfortunately revolved around a specific pair of very
good looking twins- to glare at Emily. She was flailing
her hands probably trying to get my attention. "Alex,
you're spacing out again. What's the matter with you,
mind sharing with me?" She said eying me curiously.

I looked away, but to shut her up I said, "Please
wait, only until Amjad comes, I'll tell you both together,
okay?" She stared at me thinking for a moment, then
she nodded and her facade changed back to her usual
bubbly and cheery one.

Emily is my best girl-friend. Not girlfriend. As in a
best friend who's a girl because I also have a best friend
who's a guy. My guy-friend Amjad left my old school

a year after I left but Emily stayed. According to her people stopped bullying them after I left. I don't know how to believe her. Those people literally bullied us almost all the time.

I looked at Emily who was skipping back to me with a cup of vanilla ice cream in her hand. I searched her hands for a second cup, obviously for me, and I found......nothing. I raised my eyebrow giving her an unimpressed look. "What? You were dreaming plus I wasn't bothered to ask you again so I just got this for myself." She completed her sentence by waving her ice cream in front of my eyes.

Emily is shorter than me, she's 5'3, and I'm 5'6. She has a petit figure and babyish features making her look like a thirteen or fourteen year old, even though she is a month older than me. She looks like a doll with her straight blonde locks and bright hazel eyes. Emily and Amjad have been my friends since forever. We're closer than siblings are. They both were my neighbors before, well Emily still is.

Now you must be wondering where she was last week during Sierra's birthday. Well she was visiting her grandma. I love that lady she's the weirdest but coolest grandma I have ever met in my not so long life.

"Here he comes." Emily said. We were at the airport waiting for Amjad. Our wait was over because here Amjad was, taking slow strides towards us. He looked bored but happy. A sincere smile was plastered on his face. He was wearing his all-time famous half pants with a baggy T-shirt. Amjad is an Arab but he lived out here in Canada since he was young until the last 3 years. He has a slightly tan skin, light brown eyes, jet black hair and a few stubbles making him look older than before.

He reached us and gave each one a firm handshake followed by a fist bump. He never hugged us, something about his religion. We respect it and never tried forcing him.

I grabbed Emily's arm and snatched a handbag from Amjad's. I then lead them both to my car. Okay not mine, my Dad's car. We loaded the luggage then took our seats. I started the Mini Cooper, reversed it and zoomed out of the parking lot. "So, how was life in Dubai?" I said directing my question to the one sat beside me; Amjad.

He shrugged, "The same; family gathering every week, but school is way better and much more fun." I felt happy he enjoyed his last years of school unlike I did. He must have been the popular kid, the one all girls like; at least he has the looks for it. Amjad is like my brother so no, I don't have feeling for him.

"How about we go for lunch then head to the mall." I said. Amjad groaned at the last part while Emily started jumping and clapping. "I have to take Ree and buy her a birthday gift. Please Amjad. Please." I said extending the last *'please'*.

"Okay, but only because I also have to buy her something. I totally forgot it was her birthday last week." He said. My friends love Sierra just as much as I do; since they don't have any siblings and Ree is the only kid they have ever seen growing up right in front of their eyes. Emily gave Ree her gift earlier this week so she was just going for shopping, something she loves more than life itself.

I wiped my mouth with a creamy white napkin, the taste of noodles still lingering on the tip of my tongue. "I freaking love this place. I can never ever get enough of it." I said gesturing around to the place we were dining in. We were at the most famous Chinese restaurant in our neighborhood. We caught up on the last 4 years while having lunch at our favorite place. I noticed that Emily had become more mature and Amjad's voice had become deeper and heavier. Amjad is shifting here for university. Lucky us, we've all been accepted at the same university, but of course in different fields. I got accepted in two other places too, but this one was my first choice.

We paid -each of us our own share- then left to go and pick up Ree. She must be ready by now; I called her almost an hour ago. It took us longer than usual-thanks to the traffic- but thankfully we reached before Sierra got mad from waiting. Sierra was outside playing in our garden while Mom sat in a foldable beach chair typing on her laptop. Mom and Dad have their own business; they buy old cars, repair them and sell again.

Sierra got in the backseat with Emily. She was wearing bright yellow shorts ending just above her knees and a oversized orange hoodie. She looked adorable like always. I turned around smiling at her then ruffled her extremely silky dark brown hair, the same color as mine. "So, what does my little sister want for a gift?" I asked.

"I want a big teddy bear," she said spreading her arms and extending them to her sides to show how big-a-bear she wants. "And I want it to be white with a pink bow and big eyes." She then kept on talking about what she did all day and how she finished her homework all by herself. We were all having a light conversation. At some point Amjad told Ree that he would be buying her another gift, making her squeal with excitement.

Today is the best day I've had since I came back home. It just keeps getting better and better.

I reversed the car into one of the empty slots. As we entered the closest entrance the cool air conditioned air hit my face. The tiredness of the day left my body instantly and gave me a new sense of energy for shopping. I started pulling my sister and my friends into each shop. Ree was running ahead of us, squealing at everything that amused her. Emily was walking with me; window shopping, while Amjad was dragging himself behind us, he looked bored like he usually does when we go to a mall or anywhere shopping related.

I saw Sierra stop in her tracks, staring into a shop. I think she found what she wants. I walked beside her and looked at what had caught her attention. In front of me was a zoo, not really. The place was filled with real sized animal stuff toys, giraffes with long necks and elephants with huge flappy ears. I followed Ree's stare and my eyes landed upon a very big and fluffy panda. It had black markings around its eyes and it looked exactly like a real panda just a bit more cute and huggable. We have to buy it, Ree wouldn't let it go, I know I can't and my sister's no better than me.

I walked in and asked one of the employees for help. She was a girl, around my age wearing black skinny jeans and a shirt with the shops name on it. She smiled and told me the price. It wasn't as expensive as I thought it would be, so I bought it without second thoughts. We thanked Kiera; the girl from the shop, and exited the zoo looking store. Emily was nowhere to be seen but Amjad stood there leaning on a pillar messaging someone on his iPhone. We walked down the hall looking for Emily. Don't worry, the giant stuff toy is not with us, Kiera said they didn't have a piece in store so they would deliver a brand new one to our house in around two days' time.

We found Emily in the accessories section of the mall. "Emily can't you wait for a few minutes when someone is getting something," I said with an irritated tone. She gave me an apologetic look before turning back to the earrings she was holding. She showed a pair to Sierra and said, "These would look so good on you Ree." Emily said it to Sierra but aimed her words at Amjad who looked as clueless as ever. I nudged him, "Emily is saying, that you should buy Ree those earrings," I whispered in his ear. He stepped beside my sister and asked Ree if she liked it, she nodded and handed the pair of butterfly earrings and a matching hair band to him.

Amjad paid, and then handed the plastic bag to Sierra. "Ree, I also bought you a wrist watch; a detective watch."

"I think we should head back home," just as I said that, I heard a very familiar voice or voices. I snapped my head in the direction of the voice, Ree copying my movements while my friends stood there confused by our actions. Sierra was about to shout out Fiona and Maybelle's names when I clasped my hand on her mouth and pulled everyone to a corner. Fiona and May were in a jewelry shop, the kind of shop where you give a design and those people will make it for you. They were telling the man to carve words in a ruby and the man kept refusing their request. He was saying that it wasn't possible. Fiona was arguing in a frustrated manner while May tried to calm her down.

They both turned around saying something along the lines of *'We're never coming back here'*. They left the shop turning around the corner and leaving us alone in the now empty hallway. We ran behind them, "We should follow them," I said. "Yeah, maybe they're hiding something," Sierra added.

We turned the corner we saw them turning from earlier but all we met was another deserted hallway. Where are the people, doesn't anyone shop here?! I was about to run out to look for them when someone grabbed my arm and yanked me back, "What is going on? I want to know, NOW." Emily said in a voice that gave me zero percent chances of saying no.

I took a deep breath and started explaining everything that happened last week on Ree's birthday. I told them about meeting May and then finding out she's Fiona and Jett's sister. That piece of information got a few gasps. Then I told them how Sierra got hurt and how we found a mysterious box and how Jett rudely asked for my pendant. "And then they took the box with them without a single word or explanation. I feel like murdering that stupid boy. Ugghh!!"

"I think you should go home and tell your parents what we heard back there. Maybe they would talk to their parents and ask," Amjad suggested. I think that will be the right thing to do, so I nodded and we started making our way out of the mall. I was almost near the entrance when a hand grabbed my arm and pulled me through one of the emergency exit gates.

A hand was covering my eyes leading me down a pathway. I struggled in the person's grip but did not shout. Why? It's because I had a feeling that this person, whoever he or she, are not a threat to me. We stopped and the hand fell off my face.

My mom once told me never to eavesdrop, I remember her saying, *'Eavesdropping will only lead you to problems, it's best to confront the second you hear something you shouldn't have.'* Mom was right, because the eavesdropping lead me here, to the world's biggest problem; Jett.

"What in the world do you think you're doing?" I shouted angrily. I looked around and saw my friends standing in a corner quietly. Amjad looked angry but was trying to keep his calm, Emily looked scared. "Where is my sister?" I asked, anger still lacing my tone. "She's outside with May; I didn't want her to be here." Fiona said, I hadn't noticed her until she spoke; she was wearing an apologetic face unlike her brother who looked furious. "What's your problem?" I screamed in Jett's face.

He glared, "Why were you following them?" He spat out, he looked at his sister and said, "I told you, she's lying, she knows about it."

"I know what? What is it? Tell me, Fiona you tell me, what was in that box?" I asked my voice more in control than before. Fiona closed her eyes and shook her head; she opened her grey eyes and looked at me, "We can't tell you, but we want that pendant, please, it's important to us." She literally begged.

NO, how is it important to them? It's important to me, it was the last thing my grandmother; who I was really close to, gave me. I can't just give it to them without any reason. I felt bad for Fiona and was about to give her my pendant when he decided to give his opinion.

"Give it to us, I know you know why we want it, you're just trying to trick us aren't you?" I stayed quiet, staring at him in disbelief. Is this guy out of his mind. What do I know? What the heck is he talking about?

"Jett, she doesn't know, they don't know." It was May who spoke this time. She was standing by the door, Sierra hiding behind her; probably scared from an angry Jett.

"How do you know?" Jett asked.

"I just do." That's all she said to change Jett's furious expression into a calculating one. He looked between me and May, trying to understand something I didn't know.

"I'm telling them." Fiona suddenly said, causing everyone's heads to snap in her direction.

"No, you don't. They don't need to know. Maybe her, but not *them*." Jett said pointing towards my friends, who looked just as confused as I was.

"You tell them everything you tell me, or I'll tell them myself." Jett stared at me, his eyes unreadable.

"No, I'm telling her and her friends, I think they have a right to know." Fiona said. When Jett stayed quiet Fiona let out an exhausted sigh and began telling us a tale which would change our lives forever.

Chapter 4

"Once upon a time; about a thousand years ago, there was a Kingdom. The Kingdom had a King and a beautiful Queen who seemed to have everything anyone ever wanted, but there was one thing they always longed; a child of their own. They tried everything possible and at last ended up with the fairies."

"There were hundreds of fairies, some small and some big, some ugly and some beautiful. One fairy caught their eye, she looked powerful like someone who could do the impossible, and so they summoned her."

"They told her their wish and asked her for help. The fairy told them that they will soon have a child but warned them to be careful. They took no notice of her warnings and began preparing for their newborn."

"Soon they were blessed with a lovely pair of twins, a daughter and a son. The twins grew up into beautiful adults with nobody being able to resist their charm. As time went soon the daughter, the eldest child, was coroneted as the Queen of the place. Her brother was always at her side helping her through each obstacle in life."

"Rules and regulations changed when the new Queen arrived. Life changed and not in a good way either. She became arrogant and unchallengeable, seeking the help of dark magic. She started killing people to set up her owns ways. Men, women and children died, each one a crueler death than the last."

"Then the day came when her brother stepped forward to tell her to stop but rejection was all he got. He ran away, she was too powerful for him, he could not stop her. He sought the help of his sister's maid and best friend. She escorted him out and ran away with him as she had same ideas."

"When the Queen found out she went crazy, furious, turning the world upside down........."

BAAAM!!!

"Oww, what the...?!?!"

"Alex!!! What is wrong with you?" Mom scolded, "This is the second time you've done this today."

Currently I was having lunch and it was just past noon. I had done it again, you know, falling asleep and having Fiona's voice play on a rewind in my dream. Yesterday's talk wasn't very fun; the tale was tiring, devastating yet incredible. Fiona told us an unbelievable story. A story that started like a fairy tale but this one was different; it never ended like the other ones. This tale never had a happy ending or a sad one. It just stopped in the middle; like somebody paused a movie to get more popcorn.

It was scary when Fiona told us. When she had finished nobody spoke and Emily was the first one to break the trance we had fallen in. Emily had said the exact words that were running through my mind.

"You're bluffing, right?" She had said with a look of bewilderment. We then left just asking the three siblings for some time. It was just too much to take in, too much to understand and too much to believe. They had quietly nodded; understanding the situation they had landed us in.

I wiped my face with the back of my sleeve. "I didn't sleep well yesterday, just tired." I told my Mom. We don't feel it's right telling our parents about this new piece of information. They might think we're crazy or I'm bad influence on little Ree. Last night, me and Sierra, we spent our time discussing the situation and the consequences of helping Fiona and Jett. They've asked us to meet them tomorrow; Fiona said she'd be telling us more.

I finished my meal and stood up telling everyone I'd be in my room. I nodded my head to Sierra gesturing her to meet me upstairs. I slowly dragged my tired body up the stairs and collapsed on the bed; trying my best not to fall asleep waiting. A few minutes passed and Ree walked in a packet of Skittles in her hand. She offered me some and I took willingly. She sat down beside me and leaned back placing her head on my stomach. We both stared at the ceiling; quietly listening to our steady inhaling and exhaling.

"Do you think we should go tomorrow? I mean we don't have to right?" I said to Ree. I'm sure it's not true and there is nothing to get scared of, but every time I sleep it's the same dream; Fiona's voice and blurry imaginary images.

"I think we should go, and take Emily and Amjad with us. They still have to tell us what your pendant has to do with all this." I contemplated her words for a while. Even I want to know what exactly we have to do with all this. "Again, can you tell me where you got this pendant?" Sierra asked touching the string hung around my neck. I looked down at the bright red ruby, it had weird carvings over it that were very similar to the ones on that golden box we found on Sierra's birthday. The ruby had gold trimmed around it which made it look even more attractive and aglow. The gold twisted and turned making floral shapes all around the ruby. The gold twists moved along the chain right above the oval ruby.

"I don't really remember, I think grandma gave it to me when I was little, I remember her telling me creepy stories and then one day she just gave it to me." Our grandmother was an ill lady who hallucinated and loved making up stories. I loved her and this pendant was the last thing she gave to me. I had my reasons when Jett wanted to rudely take it away from me.

"So it's decided, we will go tomorrow and ask them. Okay?" Sierra suddenly said jumping up from the bed. I looked at her, "Yeah, I think we should, but not tomorrow, don't you remember?" Ree looked at me; her face cutely twisted in confusion.

"So you don't remember, crazy, your big panda is being delivered tomorrow." I said.

"Oh right, oh my god it's going to be so much fun, where will Mr. Panda sleep?" Sierra hopped, clapping her hands excitedly; it's so easy to make her forget.

The day passed with us lazing on the couch and watching TV. Soon the moon was high up and dinner was over indicating bed time. I've been dreading sleep since morning, but I have to sleep or I'll get sick and get a fever. I changed and got under the covers, the second my head hit the pillow sleep overtook my tired system and the voices started playing.

"Rules and regulations changed when the new Queen arrived. Life changed and not in a good way either. She became arrogant and unchallengeable, seeking the help of dark magic. She started killing people to set up her owns ways. Men, women and children died, each one a crueler death than the last."

"Then the day came when her brother stepped forward to tell her to stop but rejection was all he got. He ran away, she was too powerful for him, he could not stop her. He sought the help of his sister's maid and best friend. She escorted him out and ran away with him as she had same ideas."

"When the Queen found out she went crazy, furious, turning the world upside down to find her brother. She felt betrayed that her brother left her at a time when she had all the power anyone can ask for. She sent her knights to look for him, many months passed and soon her brother was brought to the castle. He had married the maid who was now pregnant with his child."

"The heartless Queen ordered to kill her brother as he knew all her secrets and plans. She left his wife, but not out of sympathy, she let her live for her own benefit. She cursed the child to be evil; a kid whose generation would conquer and destroy the world. But, what she didn't know was that there wasn't............"

"Andy......Andy, can I sleep with you?"

I sat up, rubbing my eyes to clear my vision. Sierra was standing by my bed with a pillow in one hand and a blanket clutched in the other. She looked scared; I think she's having the same dream.

"I had a nightmare; can I please sleep with you?" Ree said climbing my bed and sitting on my lap. I looked at my side table; the digital clock on it read 05:47A.M. Mom will probably be here by seven.

"Sure, get in." I said lifting the blanket to allow her entrance. She placed her pillow beside mine and dropped her own blanket on the floor before getting under mine. I made myself comfortable and closed my eyes to find I wasn't sleepy anymore. I laid there quietly; waiting for Ree to sleep. A few hours passed -okay, just joking- after about ten minutes I heard light snores and slow steady breathing. I mean, how long does it take for a kid to fall asleep.

I slowly lifted my side of the blanket and pushed my body up trying not to wake my sister. I moved and sat in front of my study table. Opening my laptop I saw Emily online, I clicked on the request and a window popped showing a sleepy blonde on it.

"Hey, why do you look so tired?" I asked noticing her exhausted face. She turned around and stared at her mirror.

"Do I, I mean I should; I haven't slept a single bit since yesterday night." She said, "We should go and talk to them again."

"Yeah, I think we should." I said inattentively. I was distracted by my thoughts; the last words Fiona had said kept playing in my mind. I heard shuffling behind and turned around. Sierra was lying at the corner of the bed and was about to fall off.

"Just a minute," I said to Emily and went over to Sierra. I gently pulled her to the center of the bed and secured the blanket around her. I went over to my laptop to see that Amjad had also joined us on the video call. He wasn't awake if you're thinking that; Emily called him and told him to join us. He kept falling asleep every two seconds.

"So....." Amjad dragged his sentence his eyes dropping and head falling on the keyboard.

"Wake up idiot; we have to talk about this. It's important." Emily whisper yelled at him causing his head to snap up. He glared at the left corner of the screen then turned to the right looking straight at me.

"What are you going to do? I know you'll talk to Fiona and then what?" Amjad said. I haven't really decided to tell them if I would help them find the person they want. I even don't know who this person; let alone they know who this he or she is. They want us to help them find an unknown identity; someone we don't know the face of or the name of or even if the person is a male or female.

We chatted for a while, then I told them to head off to bed because Amjad kept hitting the keyboard; dozing off every minute. The last time he did that he started snoring and I had to convince Emily to go back to sleep. I closed the webcam and stared at the pink plaid screen. I repeated Fiona's words in a low voice,

"She sent her knights to look for him, many months passed and soon her brother was brought to the castle. He had married the maid who was now pregnant with his child."

"The heartless Queen ordered to kill her brother as he knew all her secrets and plans. She left his wife, but not out of sympathy, she let her live for her own benefit. She cursed the child to be evil; a kid whose generation would conquer and destroy the world. But, what she didn't know was that there wasn't one child; there were two babies; twins, which had become a trend in their family. The Queen sent her sister-in-law away with the only woman she trusted after her brother left. The lady was her one and only friend."

"The Queen gave an article to her friend and asked it to be passed down to the child born. Soon the babies were born but their aunt never knew as death overtook power and the Queen was lying six feet underground. The article which we now think is the pendant; was given to one of the babies."

"Alexandra, dear you're up early, what are you doing talking to yourself?" Mom said, making me look up from the screen which now had bubbles floating around it.

"What? Oh nothing. Just woke up, couldn't sleep." I said standing up and walking to my bathroom. I brushed my teeth and dressed in a new pair of jeans and shirt. I then walked out and went downstairs. Dad was sitting on the couch; the TV was open on a news channel and he had a newspaper in his hand. He must be leaving for work in an hour or so. I walked over to the kitchen and sat on the counter; my legs crossed.

Mom made us breakfast; Sierra woke up when Mom came into my room. Morning past and it was noon soon. The delivery must be here by one or two. We had lunch at about one thirty but the delivery was still not here. Sierra was waiting impatiently; she ran out every time a car passed by our house.

It was four by now and nobody had come. I tried calling the store but the line was busy every time.

"Come on! Dress up, we're going to go check what's the wait for." I said to Sierra who was sitting bored outside on the porch. I put on my converse and grabbed the car keys. I walked out and turned on the engine and waited for Sierra. She joined me and we drove off in the direction of the mall.

"Hello, I bought an item two days ago and it was supposed to be delivered today around one o'clock. But it never came, so can I ask why?" I asked the dark haired employee. She turned around and gave me a smile.

"Oh, it's Kiera right?" I said smiling at the girl who had helped us the last time we were here.

"Yeah, is there a problem?" She said still smiling. Her eyes drifted down to my shirt, her smile slightly faded but returned when she heard Sierra's cheerful voice.

"Can we take Mr. Panda and go home. I'm hungry." Ree said. Kiera and I laughed and walked to where Sierra was standing which was right in between a dozen stuffed animals.

"I'm sorry you didn't get your Mr. Panda, I think they had a technical problem and couldn't complete all the delivery orders." Kiera said. "I'm sure to inform them and your toy will be with you by tomorrow." Kiera completed the sentence ruffling Ree's hair.

"Thank you Kiera." We both thanked in unison and headed outside.

"She's a nice girl." Sierra said.

"Yeah, but she's weird sometimes. Never mind, we can go get ice cream and then head back home." I said. I find Kiera different and weird; like she wants to ask something but she doesn't know how.

We had our ice creams and dinner at a restaurant nearby, and then we went home to our waiting parents. Mom was washing the dishes and Dad was outside potting new plants. We went in and helped Mom; then everyone went to bed.

"The Queen gave an article to her friend and asked it to be passed down to the child born. Soon the babies were born but their aunt never knew as death overtook power and the Queen was lying six feet underground. The article which we now think is the pendant; was given to one of the babies."

"The pendant for surely was passed down the generations and is now landed in your hands

Alexandra. I don't think you're safe if it stays with you. They'll try to harm you and your family. They will come after......"

"AAAHH!!!" I woke up by falling off the bed. Did I just scream?!?!

I heard a light sob from outside. It was Sierra who had screamed; not me. I stood up and walked to her room. The door was ajar and a lamp was lit.

"Are you okay?" I asked side hugging my little sister. She clutched my shirt tightly, her hands around my waist.

"They'll come after us Andy, I'm scared." She said; her voice breaking with hiccups. Those were the last terrible and horrible words Fiona had said before leaving us to think everything over.

I closed my eyes, "I guess I'll call them and tell where we're meeting."

Chapter 5

I didn't know what was wrong with me, but I couldn't keep my feet still. Sweat beads were forming above my upper lip giving me a watery mustache. Yeah, you guessed it, I was nervous.

Why?

I called Fiona around eight or so in the morning, but guess who picked it. Jett. He, like usual, seemed annoyed and irritated at the sound of my voice. At first I considered ending the call because the idiot, also known as Jett, grunted at every word I spoke. When I threatened on hanging up he sighed and finally allowed me to speak.

That's how it went and I ended up inviting them to our house. We both agreed that this was the safest place to meet and talk. I don't know if their parents know about the matter but mine surely don't. Mom would freak out if she did.

I told Mom that everyone; who included Jett and his siblings, Amjad and Emily, were coming over. She seemed concerned for a moment but I assured her that we won't fight.

Now you might be thinking why I was nervous. After I spoke to Mom, realization hit me. The questions that had been brewing in my head for the last three days are now going to be answered. I had so many questions and queries, but what scared me were the answers. What if they cause more problems?

You know, in most cases, when long hidden secrets are spilled out disasters are ought to happen. Like when I told Mom that I was the one to break her favorite cup; even Dad hid in the garden behind his pots for the whole day. I had to handle Mom all alone which is the toughest task anyone might have ever done.

I spent the day completing chores and searching the net. Nothing helped keeping my nervousness away; even food, and that's saying something. Soon we heard a car outside and then the bell rang. I slipped on my flip-flops and descended the stairs; my phone in my back pocket.

I entered the kitchen to find everyone around the dining table snacking on fruits and ice cream. I went and sat beside Emily waiting for everyone to finish.

"So......" I trailed off as we all sat on the grass outside. Mom shooed us out the second we were done eating. We were sitting in a circle, everyone facing Fiona. She smiled at everyone and faced me.

"Do you want to ask us something?" Fiona said to Amjad who kept opening and closing his mouth;

trying to form words. He looked at me hesitantly then turned back to Fiona who was still smiling.

"Um, you said the curse was directed to one child, but there were two; so what happened after that……" Amjad asked; unsure of how to complete his sentence.

"I was waiting for someone to ask this." Jett suddenly spoke clapping Amjad on the back and causing him to bump Fiona's shoulder. He slightly blushed and moved away clearing his throat.

"The twins were born; one evil while the other virtuous. The twins were sheer opposites. They lived different lives and according to the books Dad gave us; the twins' mother died after giving birth to them. The twins were later adopted by different families in different societies." Fiona told us. "The twins' Aunt; their mother's sister gave the pendant to one of the twins and left."

"So the Queen's best friend was the twins' Aunt?" Sierra asked.

"Yes. Both of the sisters were the Queen's friends and her maids, but one of them ran away like Fiona told you before." Jett said to Ree.

"So me and Sierra, are we like from the royal family of God knows what place?" This was one of the questions that were eating my brain.

"Yes, but no. That was like a thousand years ago and nobody even knew that the Prince had kids. They were orphans remember?" Jett answered me with another irritated glance. I decided to stay quiet; not wanting to start an argument.

"How do you know all this? I mean about the pendant and all." Sierra asked.

Fiona had told us this before, but Ree wasn't with us at the time. Fiona had said something about being the descendants of the maid, the one who wasn't the twins' mother. The maid had run away with the Queen's most precious belongings after she died. She took all the spell books and antiques and travelled to a land far away.

"......and all these books and information we have has been passed down the family." Fiona explained to Sierra.

"But, we don't have everything. A lot of books were lost with time. We have a diary of the maid; but it doesn't help. She stopped writing after she left the palace." Maybelle said glumly.

"Why did you want my pendant?" I asked -my voice slightly above normal- looking directly at Jett who was pulling the grass underneath him. He dropped the green blades and wiped his fingers on his dark grey jeans. He looked up with a glare and our eyes locked. That's how a staring contest started. Neither of us wanted to retreat from their gaze.

"Guys, don't start fighting again." Fiona said causing us to look away.

"So, why did you want her pendant?" Emily spoke for the first time. She was listening intently without a sound until now. I looked at her then at Fiona; waiting for the question to be answered.

"This…" Jett stood up and walked to his car; opening the backdoor he pulled out the box we found on Sierra's birthday. He jogged back and placed it in the center. "…is why we want your pendant."

I looked at him confused.

"Give it to me." He said in a soft voice. I stared at him; finding the sudden demeanor change weird. He raised his eyebrows and gave me the *'What are you lookin' at'* look. I turned my gaze down to the grass suddenly finding it interesting. My cheeks felt warm from the embarrassing encounter. Ignoring the stupid stares from everyone I lifted my hair and tied it in a high ponytail using the band on my wrist. I unhooked the chain and brought it down to my lap. I gathered the metal chain and ruby in my fist; extending my arm I dropped it in Jett's awaiting hand.

He looked at the pendant, "Now that was easy, wasn't it?" he said with a smirk. That idiot ruined my mood with his stupid smirk. I gave him an ugly look and turned away. Fiona took the pendant from her twin and crawled to the box. Everyone followed her actions and the box was soon surrounded by seven pairs of curious eyes burning holes in it.

Jett cleared his throat, "Go on, do it."

Fiona slowly lowered the pendant on the hollow oval in the middle of the lid. The box was completely sealed from all the corners. No way to open it, no lock or button. Before she let the pendant touch the surface, she flipped it so the ruby and its carving were facing the ones on the box. The carvings on my ruby and the box were exactly the same.

She dropped the pendant and it fixed in position as if the hole was made for it. A bright red light shined from the ruby illuminating everyone's faces. We all gasped and backed away. A small click was heard and the lid popped open.

Jett and Amjad were the first ones to recover from the shock. They both moved back to their old positions and opened the box; their hands shaking in the process. The lid was thrown back displaying an old book.

The book was huge; almost larger than a laptop. It was worn from the corners and the pages were slightly wet, but it looked well enough to use or read from. Jett picked it up and placed it on the grass. There were shapes and pictures on the cover; a language only Jett could decipher. He traced the writing with his finger, reading the words in a low inaudible voice. He slowly moved his fingers to the top right corner and began turning the cover to reveal the first page.

Everyone held their breaths waiting for a surprise. I feel like laughing; I mean stuff like this only happens in movies. The cover fell to the side and the first page was filled with……..nothing. Literally *NOTHING*. It was inkless. Nothing written on it.

Jett stared at it with a blank look then turned to the next page which was also empty. He got frustrated and started turning the pages, pulling at them and trying to make something appear.

Fiona pulled the book from his hands and examined it from every corner and side. "Why is it blank?"

Before anyone had time to answer her question, a truck was heard down the street. It drove in our direction then abruptly stopped by our drive way. I instantly recognized it by looking at the huge pink-grey elephant logo on its side.

The window rolled down and the driver looked at our house number comparing it with a paper in his hands. He nodded his head towards the passenger seat and rolled the window back up. The doors on both sides opened and two sturdy, muscular men stepped out. They were wearing black from head to toe. Each and every clothing was black, even their watches. They were wearing dark sunglasses which were completely unnecessary as the sun was almost setting.

They walked to the back of the truck and opened the shutters. One of them climbed in and then jumped back with a stuffed panda in his hands. Sierra ran towards the men, Maybelle and Emily tailing behind. The man handed the panda to Ree, and Emily signed on the clipboard.

Sierra, Maybelle and Emily skipped back to us; all of them laughing on some joke Maybelle had cracked. The delivery men got back in but instead of zooming away the truck dragged along the road as if looking for something or someone. Ignoring their weird action I walked over to my sister.

"Andy, it's so cute and fluffy!" Both Sierra and Maybelle squealed in delight. They ran over to Jett and Amjad showing them the new toy. A few minutes passed with the girls running around playing and laughing with the huge teddy bear.

"I suppose we should leave now. It's getting late and I have to go somewhere tomorrow." Fiona said getting up and dusting her dress. "Come on Maybelle, we're waiting in the car."

"What about this useless book and the box?" I asked before they left. Aren't they going to take it with them?

"Keep it somewhere safe. It's not safe at our place. A lot of books we had have been disappearing recently." Jett pulled out the car keys and pressed a button. "And don't go reading it; it's no use if you haven't noticed." He said.

Obviously I've noticed. I gave him the evil eye and turned away. Stupid idiot.

"Can I stay?"

"Yes, can she stay?"

Maybelle and Sierra both said at the same time. Fiona looked at the watch on her wrist and smiled, "Okay then, we'll leave Alex in charge of May tonight." Jett and Fiona got in their car and drove off. Amjad and Emily were next to leave.

"Guys, dinners ready, come in." Mom called. We went in and washed our hands then helped setting the table. During dinner Mom kept asking what we were talking about but nobody let the secret slip. After dinner we all went upstairs, Mom and Dad headed straight to bed while the three of us sat in my room.

I had carried the box and book upstairs before dinner, don't worry, Mom didn't see me. "What should we do any ideas?" I asked as soon as we got comfortable on my bed. We ended up playing a few board games. The girls went out to the lounge.

Sierra and my rooms are separated from the rest of the house. They're -my room, Sierra's room and a small lounge- all in the far corner of the house. Nobody comes here except Mom when she has to wake us in the morning. The box was in the lounge so I went out to get it.

"I'm taking the box inside." I said moving towards the coffee table which was placed between two red couches. Sierra and Maybelle -who were sitting the couch- suddenly jumped in front of me preventing me from reaching the table.

"You can leave it here. Please. We didn't get to see it." They both said with big kitten like eyes. I don't like dogs; I prefer cats, just so you know.

"But–"

"Please. We'll keep it here. Please." They said leaving me no other choice. Anyway, nobody comes here and they can just leave it in my room after getting a look at it. I wanted to look at the book too but I was feeling too tired to even move.

"Alright, just leave it on my side table before sleeping, and don't stay up too late, sleep before one." I left the two to do whatever they were planning to.

I went and changed then went to bed. Getting under the blanket; I closed my eyes and tried to sleep. Time passed but I couldn't sleep. I heard footsteps outside and turned to look at the clock on my side table; squinting my eyes I stared at the neon numbers. Fifteen minutes to one o'clock.

"Go to sleep, it's almost one!" I yelled.

"Okay, we're just going to get some………." I heard a muffled reply, but before it completed I was already drifting off.

"Alexandra, honey, where are Sierra and Maybelle?"

"I don't know maybe somewhere out……." I slept again. God, I was so tired since the last three days.

What was Mom saying, something about where Sierra and Maybelle are?

OH MY GOD!!

She was in my room. Did she see the......

I frantically woke up; bumping the headboard in the process. Where did they keep the box? It wasn't on my side table, or anywhere in my room. I ran out to the lounge. NOTHING. Where the heck did they leave it? And where are these two?

I ran down to the kitchen, "Sierra! May! Mom!" I yelled the three names at once. My mother was the only one who replied.

"Alexandra, I can't find them. They're not in bed. It's made as if they didn't sleep last night." She said hurriedly running over to the phone. "Call Jett or Fiona and I'm calling the police for a search party. Your Dad went out about an hour ago, but he still didn't find them."

I ran back to my room, picking my phone I went to my closet. Where is her number? There it is, I hit the call button and waited. Jeans, shirt, this will be fine for today.

I ran to the bathroom, my clothes in one hand and phone held between my ear and shoulder. "Hello?" I heard a sleepy voice.

"Hey, Fiona it's Alex. Um, can you guys come over? I...um....we can't find Sierra and May. They're not here since......" The line went blank. She probably got the idea of what I was trying to say. I brushed my teeth and dressed up at top speed. I ran my fingers through my hair trying to untangle some of the knots.

Then I sped down, running to Emily's house I rang the bell, when no one answered I called her. She picked up after my fifth try. I told her everything and asked her to call Amjad who was staying at a guest house nearby.

I walked back to my house and went over to Mom; Dad was in the kitchen with her. He was on his cell phone with someone while she was on the house phone; both of them fighting about something. Mom was first to end the call, "The police is saying that they can't send out a search party just now. They said something about not before 24 hours."

I nodded and walked back out. The girls are not here and so is the box. Could it be…..maybe someone kidnapped them for something? Just then Fiona and Jett arrived, both worried out of their minds.

"What happened?" The first thing Fiona uttered in sheer panic.

"I don't know, they were in the lounge upstairs last night, and then I told them to go to their room and then I don't remember." I said earning a dirty look from Jett, most probably from the last part of me not remembering.

"Do you think it has something to do with the…… book or the box?" Emily completed the last part in a hushed voice. I turned around to see them, Amjad and Emily, walking down the road. Emily probably went to pick Amjad; his phone is mostly switched off in the morning since that day Emily called him at night.

Nobody answered her. We all went to all the possible places the girls could go, but who are we kidding, they're too young to walk around by themselves. Time went fast and we were now sitting in our kitchen; Mom talking to the police again. They finally agreed to start looking, as more than 24 hours had passed away.

Right between a nice cool drink of orange juice Amjad said something that caught everyone's attention. "How can I forget this? Hey…" He said turning to me and Emily. "Do you remember that watch, the detective one I gave to Ree on her birthday?"

"Yeah? She was wearing it yesterday." I said.

"Yes, that's what I mean. That thing has a GPS in it. We can track them down." That's all it took for all of us to start running upstairs looking for a computer or a phone.

Amjad switched on my laptop while I and everyone else started working on our phones. "I found them, they're in ………" Amjad trailed off.

I ran and looked at the screen, "How are they in…….." I paused, "Do you think it's telling us the right place?"

"Yeah" Amjad nodded.

"Where are they?" Jett asked.

I shook my head, this is impossible, "*Dubai*" I said.

Chapter 6

Okay, so how do I start?

Right now, I was in my bedroom making numerous trips from my closet to the suitcase lying atop of my bed. Mom insisted on taking a suitcase with all the necessary clothing and items like first aid and all that.

I guess you're not following me, let me explain.

When Amjad found out about Sierra and Maybelle being in Dubai; also his recent hometown, we told my parents who immediately took action. That's one of the things I love about them. My parents had a small secret talk and then Dad promptly called someone. That someone turns out to be a friend who works at the Airport. Dad asked for five tickets.

Five? For who?

Those five tickets are for:

Alex as in me, Amjad who will be our guide, Emily who was just tagging along, and the rest two for Jett and his twin Fiona. Mom is actually making Amjad and Emily go, she says something about support. Anyway, we were already planning a road trip, just the three of us; I guess it will be an air-trip this summer.

So, it's been two hours since we found out their location and there were two hours left for our flight to board. I was in my room, packing my stuff and talking to Emily through my window. Her house being right beside mines was a great advantage in times like these. We were shouting stuff like *'Don't forget your toothbrush'* or *'Do you have an extra pair of socks'* or *'Don't forget your charger'*. All that stuff.

I was only half-panicking unlike my Mom who had gone completely insane, psychotic, demented, anything you'd like to call her. She was running around like a mad woman, getting my recently dried clothes from the laundry and throwing them on my bed. Dad was talking to Jett's parents on the phone and assuring them about the tickets he had bought all five of us.

The adults were not accompanying us due to their work. Nobody was able to get an off in such short notice but us kids were fortunately on summer vacation.

Dad trusted us in situations like these; not that I've been in one before. He said we're grownups and responsible; which at least I know I am if not the others. Mom was happy that Amjad's parents will meet us when we reach the other side of the world. Of course Amjad lied, and just so you know, he was forced by the well-known Jett.

"Alexandra, come on, you're getting late." I zipped my bag and picked another smaller one. Then I went downstairs to the kitchen; bags dragging along with me. As soon as I reached the bottom, Dad took hold of my luggage, "Just going to leave it out." He told me.

I hugged my Mom and kissed her cheek, then said a *'see you soon'* and *'love you'*. Dad came in and kissed my forehead, leaving a ticklish feeling from his stubbles.

I waved to my Mom who stood on the porch, a tissue in her hand and eyes swimming in tears. Emily and I were jam packed in the back seat; the trunk was slightly empty just enough for Amjad to fit in his bag. We picked him up and our next destination was the Airport.

We got our tickets and checked in our luggage. We went through all the processes and were now seated in the waiting room. Our flight was called and we all headed to the doors.

"No I'll sit here!"

"No it's my place!"

"No, you don't have your name on it!"

"I do!"

Emily raised her eyebrows at Amjad's senseless answer. "Okay, I don't but I'm going to sit here."

"No!"

"Yes!"

"Oh shut up both of you, stop fighting like girls!"

"I am a girl."

Fiona glared at Emily and looked at Amjad whose face was completely red from embarrassment. "You sit there, and you there. And I'll sit here." She said, first pointing at the aisle seat then the one next to it and then the window seat for herself. They both pouted and took their seats. Fiona took the seat beside Amjad; a triumphant smile on her face.

Good news, I got a window seat. Bad news, unfortunately my seat was right beside Jett. But who cares, he was sitting beside an old cranky lady with a big fat purse.

As I made myself comfortable Jett walked over and opened the luggage compartment above our heads and placed in his duffel bag. "Here, keep this in too." I said lifting my rucksack. He stared at me for a moment then took the bag from my hands; placing it he closed the lid. He moved by the already sleeping lady and plopped by my side.

He was about to say something when a small *ding* was heard.

"Ladies and gentlemen, welcome abroad Emirates A380" The pilot kept speaking for a while, giving the same speech about securing the luggage and buckling the belts and etcetera.

As he kept speaking, air hostesses started displaying the safety rules. "To release the seatbelt lift the top of your buckle. Remain seated with your seatbelt securely fastened any time the seatbelt sign is on."

Our plane was huge, an airbus actually. This was the earliest flight we could find to Dubai. There were three columns in the plane, the sides with three seats; those are the ones we got, and the middle one with four seats. The plane was divided in four sections; ours was 'D'; the last one on the lower deck.

"As we come through the cabins for our final safety checks, please let us know if you have any questions. We ask again to review all the safety information from the safety regulation cards located in the seat pocket in front of you. Once again welcome aboard Emirates A380 flight 3928 to Dubai and thank you for flying with us."

The speech ended with another *ding*, and everything was quiet for a moment. The seatbelt sign lit up indicating us to buckle up. I inserted the metal tip into the buckle then pulled the strap, when I felt it tight enough around my waist I let it fall on my lap. I turned to look at Jett who was playing on his mobile.

"Tie your belt."

No answer.

I repeated my words to get another moment of silence. Getting fed up with his ignorance I slapped the back of his head.

"Did you just h–"

"Sir, can you please tie your seatbelt, we'll be taking off any moment now." An air hostess cut him off politely. He silently nodded and did as he was said. He then picked his phone and started playing again.

"Phones are not allow–" He cut me off by saying it was on *flight mode*. Stupid me for forgetting that.

We didn't talk after that, except a few sounds and grunts here and there. Soon breakfast was served. It consisted of scrambled eggs and chicken sausages. We were on an Emirati plane, that's why it said *Halal* on the side of the box, "It means that I can also eat this meat." Amjad had happily said after reading the sign.

The food was exceptionally good for plane food. The crew went around for a second time, taking away the left overs and offering drinks like tea and coffee. I was feeling too sleepy to have more food so I courteously refused the coffee I was offered.

I soon drifted off only remembering my head fall on Jett's shoulder before I went unconscious. I don't know how long I slept but what woke me up was a heavy feeling on the top of my head and the air conditioner hitting my face. Without moving, I twisted the AC knob, stopping the air, and checked my wrist watch. The long hand pointed at 6 while the small one was suspended between 1 and 2.

Wow, we took off at 4:35A.M. and it's almost 10 hours since we left Canada. Only four more hours left. I heard a light snore, someone's breath fanning my forehead. I moved Jett's head away from top of mine and placed it on the edge of my chair. He involuntarily made himself comfortable and slept on.

Stifling a yawn I unbuckled my belt. I leaned forward and pulled out a magazine, I flipped through it for a while trying to busy myself. *Shirts, skirts, dresses, more dresses............rings, earrings, pendants.* I stopped on this page, scanning it with my eyes. They're so nice, so *'beautiful'* I said my finger stopping on a bright grey one. It was circular in shape, glittery fluid filling its insides. A butterfly was inside it, silver and popping out but still inside the glass of the pendant. Silver metal strings twirled around it forming spirals on the top and bottom of its corners. It was simply beautiful.

"You like it?"

"Hmm" I answered without thinking.

Jett had woken up being the one who asked the question. I noticed he was still half sleeping. The woman beside him was snoring again and not those calm light snore but those monstrously loud ones. She kicked his leg trying to get comfortable. Jett wasn't affected by the light kick but slightly moved to my side trying to get as far away from the old lady as possible.

"You're worried what they might do to the girls." I asked speaking out my thoughts. The thought had been nagging me all day. It even gave me a creepy nightmare.

"Yes, I am but I don't think they would do anything. Probably they only want them for money or something." He said the last part more to himself.

Something. That's what's been bugging me all this time. What if this something has to do with the pendant and the book? The book was also taken when the girls disappeared. But maybe they thought the book was something important and expensive; something they can sell and earn money from. Yeah, that might be it.

"Why did you leave?"

I knew what he meant when he asked the question but I was also totally baffled. *He* is asking me *this*? When I didn't answer he spoke again.

"I know why you left and I'm sorry about whatever happened. Sorry." He repeated the apology again. I stayed quiet, mostly being speechless. Jett, The Popular Jett from when we were young, is apologizing.

I started feeling uncomfortable with the silence and decided to change the subject.

"Your birthday was two weeks ago, right?"

"Um, yeah, how do you know?"

"I was talking to Ree a couple of days before I moved here. She told me that Maybelle's brother took them out to celebrate his birthday." I paused, "I don't think she was talking about any other brother."

"Yeah, I turned nineteen. When is your birthday?"

"Soon, in two weeks' time I think." I replied absentmindedly. We were actually having a civilized conversation; no relentless arguing.

"Hello, what would you like, fish or chicken?" I hadn't noticed the air hostess until now. She stood in the aisle, the food trolley in front of her and a smile plastered on her face.

"Fish"

"Chicken"

We both said at the same time. The stewardess gave us another smile and turned to get our food. We were handed our packages and the lady started shaking the old woman who was still asleep. Gosh, how much will she sleep!!

We unlocked our food trays and started our meal. Oh My God this food is so good. The process repeated; we ate then the left overs were taken away and we were offered drinks.

Ding, just as the sound was heard the seatbelt sign went on and the pilot began speaking,

"Please fasten your seatbelts and sit back. We would be landing in a few." The short announcement like all the other announcements was repeated in Arabic.

The plane landed and I released a breath I never knew I was holding. *Ding.* "Welcome to Dubai, United Arab Emirates. The current time in UAE is 2:50A.M. We hope you enjoy your visit." *Ding.*

We pulled down our luggage and woke up the old woman who had been sleeping most of the time. She woke with a disturbing sound and grunted in response. Getting our luggage we slowly moved behind the crowd and stepped on the duct.

"Where is Jett?"

I looked around trying to spot a tall black haired boy. He wasn't there. "He must have gone inside to get something." Fiona reassured us. Jett soon walked out stuffing something in his pocket.

"Where were you?" I asked.

"Oh, just getting something."

I didn't ask again or tried to make him clarify his statement. We walked out and went through all the processes.

Let me tell you something, Dubai Airport is freaking HUGE. You feel like you're walking in a never ending place, the halls just don't stop. There is no dead end at all.

We got a Taxi, which was super easy judging by the million Taxis waiting outside the Airport doors. We soon reached our hotel, *Intercontinental Dubai*, which was in the far corner of the city.

It was a huge building, curved at the top and surrounded by water. It was stupendously lit up, every nook and cranny. The night was dark and it was shining as if all the stars have fallen on it.

"Thank you"

We said to the man who had helped us carry the luggage to our rooms. Dad had booked two attached rooms so that we can communicate at any times required. Needless to say, we were hungry; plane food is never enough. We ordered our dinner or lunch or whatever it's supposed to be. Looking at the time it's probably a midnight snack.

With our tummies full, we went to bed. How I wish my little Ree was here. I sighed, *She'll be here tomorrow............ when we find her.*

I woke up with a tickling nose and a head numbing sneeze. God these ACs will be the death of us. I climbed out of bed. Emily and Fiona were already up but still in bed. They were lying on their stomach, facing the TV and playing something. There was a knock on our and Amjad's sleepy muffled voice spoke, "Jett is going to call the room service for breakfast. Get ready and come out." Shuffling was heard and he was soon gone.

We all made a run to the bathroom, thankfully my bed was the nearest. I brushed and showered, then changing I stepped out. The girls ran towards the now free bathroom, knocking each other in the process. I opened the door and went over to the boys' side.

Jett was awake and dressed sitting on a couch with the hotel phone in his lap. His brows were furrowed and mouth twisted. He let out a frustrated sigh and looked up, "They're not answering."

"What? That can't be, this is like, one of the best hotels. Maybe you pressed the wrong button."

"No, I didn't. I called five times and they're still not answering."

Emily walked in, Fiona at her feet. They both looked fresh and cheerful; ready to head out. Emily started opening the curtains, "Stop, please don't open them. I can't bear the sun minutes after I woke."

She stopped, rethinking what I said and replying with a short nod and *'yeah me too'*. We tried calling again but still got no answer. Everyone was now in the room, our stomachs grumbling and asking for food.

"I think we should go down and check if they have a buffet." Fiona said.

"Yes, and complain about their services." Amjad added.

We walked out, well I was dragging myself. The corridors were empty and people free, we crossed no one in our way to the lifts. The view from 28 floors above ground is amazing. Tiny cars and stick like buildings looking like thousands of bamboos and tiny ants crisscrossing between them.

We entered the lift and got out in the lobby. Everything was quiet, every corner completely empty. I ran out to look for the Taxis; surely there will be someone outside. Thank God the Taxis are here, I walked closer. No one.

"Where are the people? Where is everybody?" Emily's voice echoed back from a distance.

Dubai is empty. The sudden realization hit me. *DUBAI IS EMPTY*. One of the World's busiest and nosiest city is empty and so quiet that an ant could be heard.

"This is awesome and.........scary!" Amjad's voice echoed back spookily.

Chapter 7

Sitting in a cool, refreshing lobby on fluffy sofas isn't as fun as it sounds. Well at least not in a situation like ours; I mean the place is literally lacking life.

We searched the whole hotel; inside and out. The roads, the mall, the shops; every single place is deserted. It's scary, if you ask; I have never seen something like this happen before, maybe in the movies but not in real life.

"What do we do now?" Jett asked breathlessly, everyone was tired from running around trying to find a human.

"Come out, this man won't mind if we borrow his car." Amjad was standing outside the glass doors, a key in his hand and a Taxi in front of him. Everyone stood up going to the awaiting boy and his borrowed Taxi.

On my little walk from the lobby to the door I passed a magazine rack with *'Tourist Maps'* labeled on the top in large cartoonish font. Me being me; grabbed a fistful of whatever maps I could find and ran out the door.

I climbed in after Emily and Fiona, the girls in the back and boys in the front. Amjad was driving as he was the only one with a license of this country. Well it still doesn't matter who drives, nobody is here to judge.

"Where should we go first?" Our driver asked turning around. Seriously, even I don't know where to begin.

"Just get us out of this place; maybe take us to the center of the city or near that tower. What was its name again?" Fiona said reading one of the maps I had took from the hotel.

"*Burj Khalifa*," Amjad started the car and buckled his belt. "It's near *Dubai Mall*, should we go there?"

We all nodded in agreement and buckled in for the long ride. Soon we were near the bridge separating *Deira* and *Bur Dubai,* crossing it we came in view with hundreds of tall skyscrapers. Sunlight reflected the glass buildings causing different colors to shine back.

I had tried calling but the usual cliché thing was happening; *Of course* no signal. When we gave up calling for help we switched on the GPS, which was no good either. *Please check your internet connection* it said on the blank white screen.

This is by far the worst situation I have ever landed in.

Soon we were driving parallel to the Metro track; the red route on the map. We were heading straight to *Dubai Mall* which was the next stop of the Metro;

a Metro which had also disappeared from the face of Earth like everything else in this city.

"We're here!"

The engine died down and we stepped out into the half empty parking lot. Everything looked untouched; it was as if everyone dissolved into thin air, disappeared from whatever positions they were working in.

Inside the Mall the shops were open but people were still nowhere to be seen. We walked around going through the shops; there were so many designer clothes I felt like taking. But that would be stealing and this is definitely not the right time to go shopping.

We passed an ice cream parlor, "A little ice cream won't hurt," Emily said with a cheeky grin her hand hooked above her shoulder and thumb pointing at the cream smelling shop behind her.

We all replied with a short *'yeah'* or *'okay'*. I stood behind the counter and decided to act as the Dessert Technician, supplying my friends with different flavors of ice cream. I handed everyone the flavors they like; two scoops each.

We sat in a booth enjoying the coldness of the soft creamy ice on this very hot day. The world famous Aquarium was opposite to us, but like all the other living creatures the fish in the tank had also disappeared.

"What a pity." Emily sighed, "We come all the way to Dubai and we don't get to see the fish."

"Why didn't we disappear?" Amjad suddenly blurted.

"Yeah, why didn't we?" I too was curious. Why didn't we? We are normal people aren't we?

"It probably has to do with your pendant, or maybe that we all know the history about it." Jett said, "I have no doubt that whoever did all this knows about the pendant and wants us."

Wants us or wants me? Maybe they wanted the pendant and took Ree and May with them thinking they had it. What if they wanted me and they took them?

"Who do you think *they* might be?" I asked, "I can't think of anyone."

Nobody answered me for a while; everyone trying to think if they knew someone who might do such a deed. After a few minutes of reviewing their memories, everyone shrugged or gave an *'I don't know'* or *'Can't think of anyone'*. That's how we spent most of our time in the mall, roaming around and thinking of where to go next.

We even went in *Burj Khalifa*, just let me tell you, it was the most awesome thing ever. First off, it was completely free of charge because, well you should know why. The second thing was that there were no rules, I mean; *we* were the ones making the rules in this ginormous ghostly deserted tower.

We took the lift and climbed to the highest floor possible to get. After reaching the top the view was breathtaking and thank God no one was scared of heights because this was higher than imaginable.

Don't think we were wasting time, because we weren't. From the top floor we had the view of almost everything in God knows how many kilometers around us. Everything was frozen and still; not moving from the place it was left.

Then something surprising happened making us sprint to the elevator and frantically press the 'Ground' button. This something was a train, the Metro, emerging out of *Dubai Mall* and according to the map, zooming straight towards *Jebel Ali.*

We shot through the main entrance and dashed to the Taxi we had borrowed this morning. "Where is it heading?" Our driver Amjad said.

Fiona pulled the map from my grip and straightened it out, scanning it she glanced at me, "*Mall of Emirates* is its next stop."

Reaching *Mall of Emirates* didn't take us long. Soon we were outside standing in the parking lot and staring at our surroundings. The train had disappeared again; we were right behind it thanks to Amjad's crazy law breaking driving. But unfortunately we lost the train.

"One thing I'm sure about is that that train didn't leave the Mall." I said looking around.

"We'll go in and check." Fiona grabbed Amjad's sleeve and pulled him to the entrance of the mall.

"Okay then, I'll head in this direction and Emily and you can go that way." Jett said in a leader-like tone to me and Emily. I tried not to mind his bossiness at the moment; we need to find Ree and May.

I tugged at my best friend's sleeve and nodded in the direction Jett had told us to go. He was already gone, turning the corner of the mall and heading to the side of it. We were supposed to head to the other side but I decided to go right behind the mall. When we reached the back we met a slightly annoyed Jett.

"I asked you to search the sides. I was supposed to search the back." He said irritatingly.

"You never said you will search the *back*"

"Can't you just follow simple orders?"

"Stop, please stop and just come and look at this." Emily yelled from a distance. She had-without me noticing- gone to the edge of another building east of the Mall. She was inspecting an unusual crack on the side of the glass building. They were the same shapes of that unknown foreign language.

"Come." Jett whispered lightly when he read the words.

"How did you learn to read these words?" I said without thinking. I have to stop asking question in wrong times.

Without minding my question, and that's a first, he answered me, "When my father told me about all this I went out and searched." He said without looking at me. "And that's how I ended up learning it. It wasn't as hard as it looks." He answered my unasked question with his last sentence.

"Call Fiona and Amjad, I think this is it. It will lead us to where we are headed." Jett traced the marking with his fingers.

"They'll be here, I'm telling you."

"What if they're on the other side?"

"See they are here, I told you." Fiona said to a red eared Amjad who quietly whispered a small *'yeah whatever'*.

"What are you doing?" Fiona stopped beside her twin. Her eyes widened a fraction and she turned to me. "We should follow this."

Jett nodded and we followed him. He stopped on the other side of the building and eyed a black hole in the ground. The hole was enough for an average human to fit in. Amjad stepped forward from our little group and crouched beside Jett.

"Give me your phone." Jett extended his arm to the person standing closest to him; me.

"Where is you–"

"Battery died." He cut me off, I can't actually say rudely because it's also my fault asking questions in times like this. I should really stop.

I pulled out my mobile and handed it to him; feeling very stupid. He unlocked it- just so you know; I don't have a password- and switched on the torch. The light illuminated the dark hole showing a fraction of a ladder moving downwards.

"I'll go first, then let the girls in and you can come last." Jett said to Amjad and started climbing down. My phone was held between his lips; tightly gripping it that they turned white. We slowly went after him not thinking if the ladder was strong enough. I prayed that we don't fall to our death. Soon my feet touched the hard firm ground and I steadied myself beside an awaiting Jett.

"What now?" Emily said when we were all staring at a tunnel in front of us.

"Follow the tunnel I assume." I said.

"But where will it take us." She asked her voice slightly shaking.

Amjad looked at the compass on his phone, "All I know is that the tunnel heads west."

Chapter 8

Running through a long winding tunnel; bumping around and falling without twisting your ankle are the hugest successes in life. The past hour and a half was completely uneventful, just a lot of running, pacing, walking and jogging. That's all we had been doing for a long time and by looking ahead I don't think we would be doing anything else.

It was dark but everyone had their mobiles out; using them as flashlights for light. "Can we please take a break, my legs are killing me." That was of course Emily; the biggest drama queen at all times.

So we took a break but not for too long; I had a big feeling that we're about to reach where ever we're supposed to reach. Soon we set foot into a room, not exactly, it was a junction. In front of us were three dark

93

tunnels; all heading -by the looks of it- in different directions.

"I'll go check the tunnel on the right." Amjad said.

"Okay then, Alex and I can go in the middle one and the two of you can go in the last one." Jett agreed with Amjad turning to Emily and Fiona.

They nodded and concurred with Jett's decision, and like always I didn't have a say in this. Jett grabbed my elbow and pulled me behind him, but before leaving he gave last minute instructions, "If anyone finds a dead end come back and wait in this intersection. If the others don't come back in the next five or ten minutes; go and look for them."

"Be safe everyone!" I yelled before being dragged into the darkness. My phone was with me and Jett had one of Amjad's mobiles. Amjad always carried more than one phone; he says that most Arabs will have two or more mobile, wherever they're living.

We walked and walked and walked; fifteen whole minutes of complete and utter silence. "Say something, it's getting boring with no one complaining." Jett was, to my surprise, the one to break the ice.

I thought for a moment, "I…um…you told us about things disappearing from your house?"

"Yeah, some old books and antiques. What about it?" he coolly replied not noticing my nervousness around him. I have no idea why I was nervous.

"Why didn't you report to the police…um…I mean they were stolen right?"

"Stolen…lost…I don't know, they just disappeared. That's why I told you to keep the box at your house. But now look what happened?"

"Yeah…." I trailed off. "But still, you should have told the police. Tell them it was stolen so they look for it. You could have found the culprit behind all of this earlier."

"We could have but we didn't have proof it was stolen, on the other hand, no one would go out looking for old books." He said without a glance in my direction. "And even if they found the stolen things they would ask their uses and the long hidden secret will be out in moments."

"That would be very bad."

"Yes, that's what I mean."

We stayed quiet after that, that's when we heard light shuffling and footsteps. On instinct, our guard was up and we were in ninja positions to pounce on anyone in sight. A figure emerged from a corner, tall and broad; a familiar figure. He moved towards us, casually strolling, his face still hidden from our eyes.

Jett pulled me behind him protectively. *Weird.* "Who are you?" Jett's cold tone alarmed me. Why is he being so protective and scary?

"Woah, woah, it's just me. What's wrong with you?" I know that voice.

"Amjad!" I squealed running to my best friend.

"Yeah, who else." Amjad said in a flat tone.

"Don't ever do that again!" Jett said in an exasperated voice, "I might have jumped on you or strangled you. Alex was scared." And now he's dumping his girlish complain on me.

"What?"

"I said you were…."

"I heard you the first time." I snapped. "And I wasn't scared. He was the one acting all protective like he's my bodyguard." I accused pointing in Jett's face.

"No I wasn't. I was just making sure he doesn't hurt you." I gave him a blank stare, that means the same thing you idiot; but I didn't say it out loud.

Meeting Amjad at the other corner told us that both those tunnels meet up in the same place. In the next five minutes or so we came across another room; this was an actual room, more specifically a library.

Anyone could tell this was a library with the amount of shelves and books aligned across the walls. The place was old and dusty but surprisingly it was lit. A dozen cressets were hung on the walls around us. *This is so old fashion*, was the first though that came to me. Between all the shelves was a wooden table, very much like our daily dining table back at home.

The table looked like it was dusted in a hurry; thick layers of filth still covered some areas whereas the others were laid by objects; objects and articles of completely different categories. There were a few books which was fine as we were in a library. But the confusing parts were clothes; jeans and shirts, and all different sizes too. There was a black wig and some accessories like rings and sunglasses.

"These are the stolen books. I was reading this the other day and I fell asleep. When I woke up it just disappeared." Jett was holding a dark brown leather diary. It was worn out from the corners and a few pages were hanging out displaying how old it was.

The boys were busy inspecting and examining our surroundings. I leaned over the table, making sure not to allow grime on my skin and clothes. I picked up a book and placed it on the table nearer to me; it was the same one we found in the box. I traced the shapes and writings on the cover; I wonder what they might mean?

I moved my fingers to the corner; slowly slipping them under the cover I lifted the top to reveal a blank page. "Guys come here! I found the book." They gave me nonchalant replies slightly infuriating me with their lack of concern. *Whatever.*

I picked up the book and tilted it so the page was directly facing me. Something flashed on the screen. What was that? I quickly brought the book in the same position. What was that? Before I knew it, the flash was there again. This time I picked it up; it was a reflection of my pendant.

I positioned the book so the reflection remained still and unmoving. I stared at it, the reflection was different. It was hollow instead of embossed, the insides were in a liquid state the colors swimming and swirling around the page. Suddenly the most unexpected thing happened.

The swirling colors started forming images; each image tinted with a pinch of red. They weren't any images, the colors started shaping into a figure I could recognize anywhere. *Sierra.* Why her?

The color slowly spread apart breaking the picture but then instantly pulling together into a new one. This picture consisted of my parents both smiling and happy like my sister had looked in the previous picture. This picture like the old one also broke apart and formed into Emily and Amjad.

My eyes were wide and locked on the page; my body completely unaware of my surroundings. The pendant around my neck started feeling warm; I ignored the sudden temperature change inside the pendant. The image of the pendant started glowing, sparks began flying around. Just before I caught a glimpse of Jett on the page the whole pendant fired up.

"AAHHH" The book fell from my hands and landed on the table. My body reciprocated the action and fell on the ground; I slid back, my fisted hands opening and closing trying to find protection and help.

An arm came around my shoulders pulling me to my feet and dragging me behind a shelf. I opened my eyes and jerked my hand to the pendant around my neck. It was burning my skin; I pulled it off and threw it on the floor beside me.

Jett's arm was still around my shoulder supporting my shivering body. I moved and his arm fell off. "What happened?" He harshly whispered. I know I screamed and gave away our current position but he doesn't have to be mean all the time.

I mustered the best glare I could but it unfortunately looked like I was constipated. "What happened?" Amjad said looking at the spot where the pendant was supposed to be.

Jett's fingers brushed my skin and I flinched. He immediately pulled back, his face now soft and eyebrows furrowed with concern. The said spot between my collar bones was a bright shade of red; a round spot was singed and blisters were beginning to form.

"My pendant began reflecting on the page and... and then it just blew up and flames consumed the whole thing and I screamed." I hadn't even noticed the tears pouring out of my eyes. I was sobbing and hiccupping and my heartbeat slightly above normal.

"Shhh!" Jett whispered trying to shush my hiccups. Someone was coming in; it can't be Emily and Fiona. Two men and a lady entered the library; shadows lingered on their faces obscuring them from our vision.

The men were tall and sturdy wearing black outfits. The woman was tall, around my height; her voice told us she was young. Her back was turned to us; she was wearing an off-white slightly greenish floor length dress. It flowed at the back brushing the floor as she paced from one side of the room to the other.

She was giving them instructions; her language sometimes English the other times a language I didn't understand but by the looks of it Jett surely did. His face started paling and the woman kept talking. There were moments when she was shouting at the men who were standing stoic, their heads hung low.

She said some words in a finalizing tone and walked away into the dark. I noticed that where ever they came from wasn't the same way we came from. This room definitely was joined to another place further into the tunnel.

I let out a breathy sigh, thank God their gone, it was getting hard to breathe without making sounds.

We turned to look at Jett whose face was whiter than my toothpaste.

"They were looking for brown hair." He whispered. It took us less than a moment to digest that in; and suddenly all eyes were on me, more like my hair.

"They want me."

"Yes." He looked away not meeting our eyes "And now that they don't have you, they don't need them........."

"They're going to get rid of them." I completed his sentence, my stomach dropping so far I didn't even know if it was still in my body. Dread started pooling my insides, what will they do?

Being in a situation like this, anyone would have done what I did. First, I panicked the way my Mom did when we were packing for the trip. Then I did the stupidest thing anyone can ever imagine. I ran......... I ran screaming like a maniac, I ran to the corner they disappeared from. The boys sprinted behind me trying to stop me from giving away our hideout, but right now, nothing could stop me from killing those people, whoever they were.

As I entered the next room I looked back just in time to see the boys disappear in the darkness of the previous room. I stopped. Was this the right place? Those inhumane creatures, what will they do? Those.......those.........

Before I could start a series of profanities a hand grabbed the back of my shirt and, might I add, very roughly pulled me towards them. My hand instantly flew to the back of my neck, that jerk was unnecessary. Jett could have just told me to stop.

"*That can't be Jett. He's been nothing but nice to you for the last half an hour.*" My sickly sweet subconscious spoke.

Well he snapped at me when I screamed Mr. Subconscious.

"*I'm a Miss, and that was partially your fault too. Remember that.*" He…… I mean she said again.

Whatever!

If it wasn't Jett then who was it? The moment the question registered my head involuntarily snapped up. All I met was a pair black beads staring at me with a disgusted look. That's not Jett. He's not even Amjad. He's………

"You're the……. the………" I stuttered.

"Yes sweetie, I am the delivery man from that toy store." He said each and every word slowly and carefully, as if trying not to let out too much information.

"Leave me! Let go! Amjad help!" Jett's voice bellowed throughout the cave-like underground rooms. He was unlike me, trying to fight the other sturdy delivery man who kept his hold firm on Jett's T-shirt.

"Son, please stop moving, you'll get yourself hurt. Please. Stop." Wow! First he holds him in a death like grip and them he calls him *son*. Just wow!

The man who was holding me moved, dragging me with him, and caught Amjad's shirt in his big meaty hands. "Let go!" Amjad screamed in surprise. He had been trying to free Jett and the sudden smack on the back caught him off-guard.

Great! Please note sarcasm. My stupidity has got us caught. I should really stop talking *and* acting at wrong times.

"Well, well." A very familiar voice said. "I knew you would need guidance." She laughed. "Boys bring them here."

My breath caught in my throat. She can't be the other heir. Well not the heir, I mean, like Jett said *It was a thousand years ago.* But.........

"Kiera........" My voice came out less than a whisper. I can't act weak at a time like this.

"But your hair it's not black..........it's...." Her hair......it was black but now it's brown. Well that explains the wig. She was wearing a wig to stay hidden. Her brown hair; the exact same color as mine, and her green eyes; the exact same shade as mine, they are the biggest give away. Now, when I look closely, she looks a lot like me.

"What guidance?" Jett shouted.

"Ha-ha, you're just too funny. You don't call that Metro guidance." She sneered. "You know, its human instinct; to do foolish things."

We stayed quiet which of course she thought was a sign to keep talking, "So what do you think I should do with them?" She pointed to a corner. "Should I let them dehydrate like they already are, or should we bury them alive?"

"Shut up! Stop this, they don't have anything thing to do with you. They're just kids." My voice slightly cracked on the last words. How can someone be so heartless?

"Not my kids." She shrugged as if it was no big deal. "Oh, oh, we should definitely break their necks and let them die. Just imagine that sweet musical sound. *SNAP!*" She clicked her fingers and I felt bile rising in my throat. I think last night's dinner is deciding to make reappearance.

"Oh, what is this? The pendant I've wanted since I saw you." Kiera's words were directed to me but her eyes were locked on the pendant clutched in Amjad's hands.

"Why did you bring it here?" I tried my best not to choke on my own spit when the man bumped mine and Amjad's heads together.

"Do that every time she tries to talk." Kiera commanded.

"Give it to me." She said to Amjad who didn't dare look up. She lifted her hand and brought one finger to Amjad's throat. "Give it to me." She said again, her finger was pushing onto his throat and a small cut started forming where her nail was.

"NO!" Amjad yelled. He's a brave guy but now is not the time.

"Amjad give it to her." I pleaded. "Please." He looked up at me and closed his eyes. He then handed the pendant to the cruel girl who once again started laughing with a mocking tone.

She walked away leaving my best friend to breathe normally. She pulled at a string around her neck and revealed another pendant. It looked exactly like mine except it was blue.

I looked around; this was the first time I decided to look around. This room like the library was also dimly lit. There were a few steps in a corner which led to a higher ground; a chair was placed above.

As I scanned the room my eyes landed on two innocent little girls. Sierra and Maybelle; they were both unconscious and dehydrated. Their faces were a pale yellow and hands were tied behind their backs. They were sitting on two wooden chairs; their backs facing each other.

"No look what I'll do." Kiera said causing me to look at her. She was now standing on the stairs. Both of the pendants were in her hands and she was rubbing them together saying words me and you both didn't understand.

A pain started forming at the back of my head. The man's grip on my shirt loosened and I involuntarily started walking towards Kiera. The pendants in her hand dissolved into each other and combined into one.

A purple pendant.

She hung it around her neck, and it perfectly fit between her collar bones. It was beautiful; my favorite color too. The color inside the pendant swirled like they did in the book.

As she kept saying the words I felt a rush of air behind, but I was too distracted to look who or what did it. I felt slapping sounds behind me but nothing could stop me from staring at Kiera.

Her eyes were closed and she was saying words I never understood. Smog started appearing around her; black and cloudy. It surrounded her and kept floating around her. The scene was hypnotizing. She was being lifted in the air; slowly off the ground and into the black darkness of the smog.

"HEY!?!" Jett yelled from behind me. I turned around and Kiera's eyes opened.

The scene played in front of me like a terrible nightmare. As she opened her eyes she was shocked. Jett stood in front of her; heaving and breathless, his eyes cold and deadly, in his hands was the book. The book that burned my skin. The book that wanted everyone I loved dead.

She let out a scream and I saw droplets of blood fall down from under the purple pendant. I turned around and looked at the book. There it was, her biggest fear; dying.

She was dead the second the pendant reflection got stabbed. Her head hit the floor and she stayed still. So it's over, that's it. She's dead. I, like always, said it a bit too early. The walls and floor began to shake; everything...

"The place is coming down!!" Jett yelled, still slightly breathless. He helped Amjad who had- I don't know when-fainted. He together with the other men was lying on the floor rubbing the back of his head.

The man who had caught me ran for his life; he sprinted to the library and was soon gone. That only left us to die here or run behind him. Of course we did the latter but not before we untied our sisters and carried them with us. Jett carried Maybelle while Amjad helped him. The other man helped me carry Sierra. At least someone is not that heartless.

We ran out as fast as we could, we passed the library and were now near the intersection. That's when we heard a loud scream, "Fiona is that you?" Jett shouted and his voice echoed back.

We moved forward and Fiona came running towards us, "Guys, that wasn't me. I think that was Emily." Emily?

"Where is she?" I couldn't help but ask.

"We thought we should look for you guys so I took this tunnel and she went in the oth….." Her voice blocked out and I was soon zooming out of this tunnel to the intersection. I reached there in less than a minute and took a U-Turn. Entering the tunnel Amjad had gone through before; I sprinted looking for the petite blonde.

In a matter of five minutes I had reached my destination. The walls all around us were cracking and tumbling down. The ground was slowly turning into moving sand, starting from the place Kiera lay in that room towards us like a snake slithering on cold wet grass.

The man who had run away before was clinging on Emily's arm. One of her feet was stuck in the moving sand. He was trying to pull her down in the sand with him. Half his body was already buried and it looked as if she had tried to help him but had fallen in his evil trap.

"Alex, help me!" Emily shouted. Tears were streaming down her face as she clung to a rock for her dear life.

"Wait." I pulled at her leg but nothing budged. The man was going down fast but there was no use helping him, it was too late for the poor guy. I tugged at Emily's leg which was very slowly and smoothly beginning to be buried under the sand.

The man let out a loud shout and his head disappeared under the killer sand. Emily was now crying her eyes out as she gripped on my shoulders. Tears were running down my face.

I heard a sound behind me and saw Jett searching. "Here, help me!" He ran over and grabbed Emily's leg while I held her shoulders. Together we heaved and pulled and thank the God she was out.

Jett guided us out of the tunnel; Emily limping as she had lost one shoe and I was heaving from the heavy lifting. The pain in the back of my head hadn't subsided yet; it was growing worse every minute.

As we ran the sand neared us more and more; moving smoother, steadier and faster than water. We moved out into the junction. The middle tunnel was already blocked as was the tunnel that lead us to this junction. "This way!" Jett leaded us.

As we stepped in the third tunnel I came in sight with Fiona. She was standing on a pile of stones waving us to move behind her. As we moved forward I saw light and noises. We climbed out of a hole hidden behind the pile of rocks and came in view with a very busy Metro Station.

"Everything is finally over." I sighed.

"Ha, look at them saying they're late for work." Jett pointed out a man in a suit with a briefcase in his hands.

I felt the sharp pain again. I looked up and saw Jett rubbing the side of his head, the voices and sounds slowly started blocking out. I yelled his name but he didn't respond. He fell to the ground and remained still.

This was the worst feeling ever. A feeling when your body goes completely numb; petrified. You feel as if your body parts aren't in your control. They feel like they're constricting; pulling in. And the worst part is that you don't know where that *in* is. Sometimes it's as if they are going right into your body but sometimes it's like your skin is pulling tightly around you; holding you captive in a cage you feel like you can never escape.

That's how I felt when I saw Jett falling down; not waking up when I called him. Another sharp pain hit my insides. It slowly got blurry and everything disappeared.

That's when I realized.......

Feelings change: like my hatred changed into love.

Chapter 9

I turned to my side; my eyelids shut and mind wishing for the throbbing pain to get over. The pain; it's intense and doesn't leave me. How did I get it again?

As I jogged my memory the images and scenes started to repeat. Oh my God. I fainted and Jett...... is he alright?

"Jett, stay in bed!" Fiona sounded frustrated and tired. "You were unconscious for two hours. Don't you understand? Get back in bed!"

"I'm hungry! I want something to eat, can't you be useful and make me something!" Jett exclaimed.

A smile formed on my lips as I heard the chattering of my friends. My eyes were heavy and my head still felt foggy, but I still managed to open my eyes. "Oh, hey, Alex is up!" Jett shouted when he saw me sitting up. He was standing in the doorway, trying to balance a soda and two large packets of chips.

As soon as everyone heard him they hurried into the room, knocking Jett in the process. He choked on the soda causing everyone to laugh. His face scrunched and he grumbled calling us *'idiots'*.

"Jett, how are you?" I said in a hurry. "You fainted and it was terri–"

Before I could complete, a smirk formed on Jett's face "So, you were worried?"

"Of course I was. People don't just faint, you know." I exasperated. He didn't reply but it wasn't hard to notice the amused smile on his face.

"Emily, are you okay?"

"I'm fine Alex; does your head still hurt?" I stared at her. The way she cried when I reached to help her was heart-breaking.

"But I feel bad for that man. He drowned in sand, that's just–"

"Emily!" Fiona said, "He tried to kill you to save himself. How can you feel *'bad'* for him?" Fiona looked angry and tired. Her hair was messed up as though she had been pulling at it.

"Alex, remember the pendant Kiera had?"

"Yeah, the blue one?" I still was curious about the matter, "What about it?"

"You know how she got it?" I looked up at the doorway. Leaning on the frame was the man who helped me carry Sierra. Sierra?!?!

"Sierra and Maybelle….where are they?"

"They're fine; I gave them some medicine and told them to sleep. They were just a bit dehydrated and hungry. I called the parental and told them, so don't worry." Fiona yawned and climbed on the bed sitting beside me.

"And why is he here?" I asked pointing at the man.

"Gary." I stared at him; confused. "My name, it's Gary. And you won't be here if I wasn't there to carry you." He states matter-of-factly.

He looked like a good person, the operative word being *like*. "I tried to sneak in some food for the girls but those idiots were always around." Gary said referring Kiera and the other man as idiots. He walked into the room and crowded around the bed like the others.

Amjad and Jett had pulled chairs and were sitting beside the bed. Fiona was on the bed beside me and Emily was at my feet. Gary just stood there awkwardly not knowing what to do and what to say.

"Thanks for trying." I mumbled still feeling tired.

"Jett." I said looking at him.

"Yes?"

"How did you get the book?"

"When she started saying those words, I knew something would happen. Gary's grip on my shirt loosened and I sprinted out to the library."

"Why did you let him run off?" I turned to Gary with curiosity.

"Oh, he didn't let Jett run away. We fainted, all of us who were in the room at the time." Amjad explained.

"But I ran out in time." Jett said with a smug grin.

I rolled my eyes, "I didn't faint."

"It was probably because Kiera didn't want you to faint, but let me remind you. You were completely hypnotized and only snapped out of the trance when I yelled."

"But how did you know the book will kill her?"

"I knew it from the day we opened the box." Jett said.

"*WHAT!?!?*" We all shrieked.

"Okay, not really. But I saw what the book did to Alex and I already knew what it was meant for."

"What was it meant for?" Emily asked leaning forward like a secret was about to be revealed.

"The cover, remember there was something written on it...." We all nodded, even Gary did who I don't think exactly understood what we meant.

".....yeah, well what written on it was......" He paused for emphasis, "Desire and Trepidation."

"But when I looked at the book I saw..." I tried remembering what I saw.

"You saw......." Everyone leaned in like Emily had done before.

"I saw Sierra and Maybelle, my parents and my friends. I also saw Je...." I stopped mid-sentence. Now is not the right time to say this.

"And who?" Jett asked.

"No, no, no one." I tried reverting the direction of our conversation. "And then..... they all burned up and vanished into flames." I said remembering the horrible feeling of losing everyone.

"Don't you understand?" Jett said while everyone stared at him with confused expressions. "You wished.......desired that your family and Sierra were with you....." That's right; I do remember being worried about Sierra.

"...and my fear is to lose them." It was making more sense now. Kiera saw herself in the book when Jett held it in front of her. She saw how powerful she will be and then she saw her worst fear. She died the second the purple pendants reflection was stabbed.

"My skin burnt when my pendant burnt." I touched the blister on my neck and winced. Taking in a sharp breath, "And Kiera got stabbed when her pendant got stabbed."

"Gary you were saying before. Where did Kiera get the pendant?" I asked Gary who had gone out to check on Ree and May.

"Where did Kiera find it?" He said with an amused expression, "More like where your sisters found it."

"What do mean?" Fiona asked. Oh, so no one had this conversation before.

"You know we kidnapped the girls." We nodded. "When we reached your house we found them in the kitchen, they had a knife in their hands and were trying to cut the book."

I gasped, "Why?" I closed my eyes trying to remember what I heard that night, *'Okay, we're just going to get some..........' I heard a muffled reply, but before it completed I was already drifting off.*

"They must be playing with the book and heard something move inside it......."

"Yup, so they tried to cut the cover and find out."

"Did they cut it? May can't even hold a knife." Fiona asked eagerly.

"No, Kiera opened it when she forced the secret out of them. She took a cutter and slashed a small cut on the spine of the book. And voila, a shiny blue pendant jumped out." Gary explained; his eyes were fixed on the ceiling probably thinking of the last few days.

"Why *Dubai*?" Jett asked causing Gary to look at him. "Why not Canada or anywhere nearer to home?"

"*Dubai* is what's nearer to home for Kiera?" We stared at Gary. What does he mean? "Kiera's mother is an Emirati and *Dubai* was her hometown. That cave was an old hideout for her family, her parents and her cousins."

We all talked for some time. Lunch time neared and Fiona called room service. Thank God, this time the call was immediately answered. Soon Sierra and Maybelle woke up and joined the lunch.

"Gary," Emily stared at him, "You kidnapped the girls, right?" Gary nodded so Emily continued. "How did you bring them to *Dubai* this fast and without their passports?" Even I was wondering about this. We all dropped our burgers and fries and stared at Gary for an answer.

He completed his bite chewing on it slowly making us immensely impatient. "I have a friend; a very rich guy." He chewed again. "He has a house back in *Canada*, and another house in *Dubai*." He paused. "I asked him a favor and he lent me his private jet without questions." Gary shrugged as if it was no big deal. I already hate this friend of his.

I cleared my throat trying to break the tension. "So Gary, do you…..um…..really work at that toy store in *Canada*?" I wasn't sure how to ask the question without showing that I thought he was a liar about not telling us the last news earlier. He had contributed a large part in the kidnapping.

"Yes I do work there. I'll be leaving after lunch; I have to make a call and tell them I was sick and couldn't make for the last two days." Gary added a last part telling us he'll leave after Lunch.

After lunch we all got in our beds for a nap; today was the most adventurous and exhausting day in my life. "How did you find the hole to the Metro Station?" I asked Fiona and Emily who were, once again, lying on their stomachs playing with something on the TV.

"We were just strolling, staring around and talking about fashion and arguing about which show is better. Alex which one do you think is better, Ameri–"

"Emily, focus! What did I ask you?"

"How did we find the Station?" She mumbled feeling low because I cut her off.

"Emily, so how did you?"

"Ask Fiona."

I rolled my eyes at her childishness, "We, like Emily said, were.......talking," Fiona was about to repeat Emily's words but stopped when I gave her a blank stare. "We heard a train and tried to near the sound. We figured it was coming from the other side of the wall." This must have been when Kiera fell down and the spell she put over the city broke off.

"So we tried to hit the wall, and fortunately it crumbled down. I was almost going to be buried under the rocks." Emily continued.

"So when I found you in the tunnel, it was the second time you were going to be buried." I said with a laugh. They laughed with me and I felt all the exhaustion and weight lift off my shoulders.

Finally we can enjoy our summer like normal teenagers.

Chapter 10

Two weeks later
"HONK!"
"HONK!"
"HONK!"

The curtains were drawn but the early rays of sunshine were peering through the tiny gap I had unfortunately forgotten to close.

"Ignore the sound and keep sleeping. Remember how late you slept last night. Keep sleeping." My subconscious was irritating me to no extend.

Sun blinding your sight, car horns deafening your ears and having a senseless mental debate with yourself is not the best way to wake up on your own birthday.

It had been a week since we travelled back to *Canada*. The remaining days of our stay in *Dubai* were spent shopping and watching movies at those glorious cinemas. We didn't hear from Gary only until three days ago. He called us to tell us that unlike him the other guy and Kiera had quit from the job and that their disappearance wouldn't be a problem as long as their families don't contact. It still didn't matter, nobody had proof we were present when they disappeared, more like died.

"*HONK!*"

My subconscious tried to make me *keep sleeping* again, but I had had enough. I sat up and tied my disheveled hair into a messy bun. I straightened my shirt and climbed out of bed. Rubbing my eyes I stomped out of my room heading straight to the kitchen where I hoped breakfast would cheer me up.

The house was empty, Sierra's room was open and the bed was made. I called to my parents but no one answered. Oh my God, what if everything is repeating? I shook the thought when I heard my mother calling me outside.

My eyes were crusty from sleep and my senses were working very slow. In front of me were my Dad and my Mom and my sister; all of them dressed up and ready for the day.

"What's all the honking about?" I said still trying to open my eyes completely. "And why is everyone dressed?" My eyes ponderously adjusted to the car behind them.

"SURPRISE!"

"Happy birthday Sweetie!"

"Happy birthday Alex!"

"Happy birthday big sister!"

This was the biggest surprise of my life. "Is that for me?" I asked breathlessly staring at the beauty behind them.

"It's all yours." Dad jingled the keys in my face and grinned. I snatched the keys eagerly and ran to the car. It was an Audi, "Is that Audi A7?"

"Yes it is. But you're not riding it now. Breakfast first." Mom said when she saw me getting in and ready to drive off. I bopped my head and locked the car. Together we walked in and dropped on the chairs in the kitchen.

"Go brush your teeth and get ready." Mom said to me as I was the only who wasn't ready for I don't know what.

"We invited all our friends for a small party. So go and get ready because you're driving unless you want me to." Sierra grinned mischievously at the last part.

"Not happening." Mom said with a chuckle and Ree's face dropped. As if we'll let a ten year old drive.

I brushed my teeth and dressed into my usual jeans and shirt. I grabbed breakfast from the kitchen and made myself a cup of coffee. Then I walked out to the living room where Dad was reading the newspaper and Mom was catching up with the shows she had missed due to her very busy business.

"Where's Ree?" I asked when I finished my pancakes. I downed the last drops of my now cold coffee and placed the now washed and clean plate and cup in the cabinet.

"I'm outside waiting for my crazy sister." Sierra yelled from our front yard. I picked my car keys from the counter and shouted a *'see you later'* to my parents who were unfortunately not going with us because it was a working day.

I sneaked behind Ree and started tickling her sides. She laughed and squired in my grip, "Whose crazy?" I laughed.

"You!" She wriggled out of my grip and lied on the grass trying to breathe steadily. I lied beside her staring at the cloudy blue sky. A light breeze was playing and the day felt perfect.

"Where is the party?" I asked after a small moment of silence.

"At the one and only lagoon."

"Why there?" I said feeling a bit uncomfortable about the idea.

"It's a beautiful place and you can't just not go there because of some stupid box." She was right. Sierra got kidnapped and if she can think positive so can I. Just like that all negative ideas left my mind and I stood up.

I offered my hand to my sister and pulled her to her feet. "Come on then." I said cheerfully, a genuine smile forming on my lips.

I parked the car and jumped out, "Get the basket from the back." Sierra shouted from the passenger seat.

"What basket?" I said opening the door to the backseat to check what she was talking about.

"Mom packed it in the morning. It contains all the snacks and drinks we would need for this small party." Sierra walked to the hut and stood on the front steps looking around at the beauty of this place.

The place was still as captivating as before. Everything was still and unmoving, well everything except the water and the occasional birds and crickets.

I picked up the basket and saw my laptop lying beside it. "Why is my laptop in the car." I shouted to Ree.

"I thought we could watch a movie before everyone arrives." Sierra said when I got inside the hut.

She ran over to the couch in the corner and snuggled in it, "Did Dad tell you he bought this place so we can come here as much as we want."

"Really?!?"

"Yeah! I guess that was another surprise."

We spent the next hour watching a movie. Dad bought furniture for the hut so we were comfortably seated in a fluffy leather couch. I paused the movie and stood up stretching my arms to release the stiffness, "I'll get more popcorn."

I filled the bowl with more popcorn that Mom had also packed with all the other snacks. "Come on, start the movie." Sierra said clapping excitedly.

I sat on the couch and reclined back making myself comfortable. Sierra climbed on the back of the couch, her back against the wall and legs dangling on both my sides. She leaned over my shoulder to get a better a better view and her fists involuntarily began kneading my shoulders.

I relaxed and resumed the movie. It was an old movie about a group of explorers who go on an expedition, in the end they end up in a *Pyramid* in *Egypt*. I watched as the movie slowly came to an end, the explorers ran out just in time to see the giant *Pyramid* turn into sand; thin and watery.

As the scene played the memories returned. The day in that underground tunnel was coming back to me. The moment everything came tumbling down I knew it was over. The history we had resumed had now come to a stop. The movie had finally ended as where the popcorn.

I watched the credits roll up and the theme song play. I closed the window and shut down the computer. In no time Emily arrived and helped us set up the snacks, plates and cutlery. We placed the drinks on a small table like we had done on Sierra's birthday four weeks ago.

Sierra and Emily went out to collect pebbles and stones to make a castle. Amjad arrived and Jett, Fiona and Maybelle did after him.

We soon gathered around a round table and I cut my cake which had a huge nineteen creamed on it. I stepped back and Sierra jumped on my back shouting *'Happy Birthday'* again and again.

"Here's your gift!" Sierra said jumping off my back. In her hands was a small red ring box. In the box was a pair of tiny diamond earrings buried between a plush white silk cloth.

"Thank you." I bent down and kissed her cheek. Mom and Dad must have bought it for her. Money has never been a problem to our family, in fact we've always had more than necessary.

Emily gave me a pair of designer boots, "How did you know I wanted these?"

"I saw you eying them when we went to the Mall to buy Ree's birthday gift." Emily said.

Amjad gave me a card with a poem written inside it and an envelope with money. "You've been giving this to us since we met." Emily and I said giving him a blank look.

"What? I don't know what to get a girl." Amjad said putting his hands up in defense.

I thanked both my friends and started cleaning up the table. "Hey! We have a gift too." Fiona and Maybelle said at the same time. I bent down to Maybelle's level and smiled.

"So......"

"Here, this purse is from me and whatever's inside the purse, is from May." Fiona handed me a white purse wrapped in clear plastic. It had a bow on the front and a shiny glass crystal in the middle of the bow. I twisted the crystal and a click sounded. I opened the purse and peered inside at a cuboid box cover in pink wrapping paper.

"That's from me." Maybelle said cheerfully a wide grin spreading across her face.

I tore the cover and uncovered the box, inside was a group of key chains. A purple fur ball key chain caught my attention and I pulled it out. "For your car key." Maybelle said.

I laughed and pulled out my car keys to attach them to the key chain. I thanked the girls and soon the hut emptied as everyone moved out.

"I got you this. I think you'd like it." Jett's voice startled me causing me to jump in surprise.

"What?!" I asked in a surprised tone. Jett bought me a gift. *WOW!!!*

I took the box from his hands and opened it. Perched in the middle was a pendant, and not any pendant. It was the pendant I saw in the magazine on the plane to *Dubai*. That explains where Jett disappeared when we got off.

I smiled, "Thank you."

"So we can be friends now?" He asked; his face twisted into hope.

So he wants to be my friend, should I tell him I already forgave him or should I make him squir–

"Stop making that face, you're creeping me out!" Jett shuddered. I looked at him; confused what he was talking about, "You're thinking of taking revenge, aren't you?" He asked with a slightly sad tone.

"Me, revenge, no," I said in an exasperated tone while pointing at myself, at which he chuckled. I made a thinking face then extended my arm to him; he stared at my hand with a confused expression. "I…um…let's start over?"

He frowned staring at my hand, then -to my relief- slowly started nodding in agreement. I let out a joyful sigh, "Hello, I'm Alex?"

He shook his head and smiled, "Is that a question or a statement?"

"Just go with it!" I snapped folding my hands.

"Okay, okay," Jett raised his hands in defense, "Nice to meet you Alexand–" And I punched him, "Hey! Why'd you do that?" He scowled rubbing his arm.

"It's Alex."

He stared at me and -once again- shook his head, "Nice to meet you Alex, this perfection in front of you is known as Jett." He said with a smug face. "So... would you like to be friends with me-the-great?"

I chuckled, "I'll think about it."

I took the pendant out of the box and unhooked the lock on the chain. I tied it around my neck and looked up to a smiling Jett.

"Let's go out and see what everyone's doing." I said.

I walked out to the front steps, Jett's hand slipped into mine and I smiled at him. I looked around and a flutter settled inside if me. I felt happy.

You know of the saying *'Take a picture; lasts longer'*.

Well this was a moment for a perfect click. Amjad and Fiona holding their drinks and laughing like there's no tomorrow. Emily being the most playful nineteen years old in this world, playing with the girl I love and the girl I love loves. My Sierra and Jett's Maybelle.

I looked up at Jett. My fears and nightmares were gone; he was the one who conjured them and he is the one who took them away. My trance broke when I noticed a smile forming on Jett's lips.

Yup, this is the most perfect moment in my life so far.

Acknowledgements

I, Sarah Syed the author, would like to acknowledge:

- My parents for supporting me on every step towards the publishing of this book.
- My little brother Ahmed for his funny comments and meaningless ideas.
- My two best friends, Manar Al-Hashar and Massara Zidane, for being my first and most trusted readers.
- My uncle Akhtar Naveed for encouraging me to express my thoughts.
- My cousin Shaima for liking my ideas and thoughts and for being honest when it came to comments.
- My family, friends, teachers and Qurum Private my school.

About the Author

Sarah Syed is a young author and school student. She is originally a Pakistani but was born in 1998 in Oman where she currently lives with her parents and brother, Ahmed.